SHENANIGANS
WHEN DECLAN MET MARY

LACYNDA MATHES

World Castle Publishing, LLC
Pensacola, Florida
Copyright © 2025 Lacynda Mathes
Hardback ISBN: 9798312445046
Paperback ISBN: 9798891263567
eBook ISBN: 9798891263574
First Edition World Castle Publishing, LLC, March 17, 2025
http://www.worldcastlepublishing.com
Cover: Cover Designs by Karen
Editor: Karen Fuller

Author's Note:

Dear Reader,

Thank you for entering my world of romance, intrigue, and mystery. I hope you'll love Dan, Miranda, Gavin, Deb, Declan, and Mary as much as I do.

My novels build upon each other, so it would be helpful, though not necessary, to read them in order.

- Forget Me Not
- Forgive Me Not
- Forsake Me Not
- Murder and Lyrics
- Homecoming
- Ghosts
- Shenanigans: When Declan Met Mary

I dedicate this manuscript to my family. You are my inspiration in all things. I love you with all my being. Happiness is easy.

PROLOGUE

June 10, 2008

Declan and Father Murphy watched as the tiny casket was lowered into the grave. Declan had only felt this alone one other time in his life. That had been the day his mother had been memorialized. There was no body or casket then. She had been reduced to DNA.

He hadn't told his family about Jess, her existence, let alone his marriage to her. She was 16. He was 17. They were too young. And he didn't even much like her. He'd agreed to the marriage only because she was pregnant, but she seemed dead set on destroying the child. In the end, she had, but not before destroying herself. The child outlived her by 7 days and 14 hours.

He'd suffered those 7 days and 14 hours of hope, fear, and dread as a penance…or a glimpse into hell…he wasn't sure which. He'd loved the tiny baby girl from the moment he'd seen her. He'd never love anyone else this deeply.

He sang *Red is the Rose* softly, mournfully as the coffin was lowered, fighting the tears.

Declan slowly became aware of the girl standing just to the side and behind him. She was dressed in jeans and a pink tee shirt with a sparkling rainbow behind a majestic unicorn galloping across her torso. She held out a single red rose to him as he finished singing. "For your daughter," she said softly. Clearly American. She was dressed like a child, but she had the body of a teenager. Based on that dichotomy, he'd guess she was 12 or 13, an early bloomer. Cute as a bug.

"And how de ye know this is ma daughter?" he asked.

"Well, the song is for a girl. If it were a boy, you'd have sung *Danny Boy* or something. And you're young to be a dad, but you're here alone. If this were a sibling, your parents would be here. But if the baby was yours, then it's possible you're having problems at home. It's a guess, but it's a good guess. I'm sorry your baby died."

"Thank ye. It is a good guess. Ye're right. Ye're a smart one, aren't ye?" Declan said, sniffing and taking the rose.

"I'm told I'm precocious," she replied.

"Aye, dat ye are," he agreed.

Her family called to her from across the graveyard, and she waved and ran off, leaving him alone again with Kathleen Orla and Father Murphy. Declan felt a tear run down his cheek as he tossed the rose into the grave.

CHAPTER 1

November 11, 2025
Donaghmede, Dublin, Ireland

Maggie McIntyre picked up the last of the children on her bus route at 8:10 am and was less than a kilometer from St. Francis of Assisi Primary School when the Ford Fiesta cut her off. She slammed on her brakes to avoid hitting the vehicle. A Land Rover behind her stopped, and the driver and passenger both opened their door and pointed semi-automatic weapons at her school bus. The driver of the Fiesta in front of her did the same thing. The passenger of the small hatchback had a weapon as well. But he came running at the school bus. At the door, he slammed the butt of his gun against the glass and demanded Maggie open the door. She did as he commanded.

As a reward for her compliance, he forcibly pulled her from behind the wheel and flung her out the door on her head.

She struggled to a seated position in the middle of the road to watch as the two vehicles and her bus full of primary school students drove off and past the school.

She thought she was seeing things when a man ran into the street and at the bus. In her 62 years, she'd never seen a man chase down a speeding bus on foot, let alone a hijacked one. Somehow, not only did he catch the bus, but he forced open the door, and seconds later, the man with the weapon was flung from the moving bus, and it came to a stop.

"Did ye see dat?" she asked the man who stopped to help her up.

******

May 11, 2026
Arlington, VA, USA

Mary looked at her reflection in the mirror. She looked tired. Of course, she did. The twins had been up half the night. Randy had a fever. His sister wouldn't sleep unless it was with him, and Mary couldn't risk Dani catching the flu, so she had to keep them apart. Even the slightest illness could be life-threatening for her daughter. Dani had been the smaller of the two, and she'd gotten an infection shortly after birth. While she was healthy now, almost 3 years later, Mary wouldn't risk her health for a night's sleep.

Unfortunately, today she was meeting her new boss. A week ago, she'd been reassigned from working as the Executive Assistant to Howard Fox, a founding partner at Fox, Goodwin, and Kane, a law firm in Arlington, VA, that specialized in international law, to a new envoy from the London law firm they were partnering with to work with the Grand Egyptian Museum on reclaiming several appropriated Egyptian artifacts from museums around the world. It was a demotion. But at least she'd held onto her job.

Being a single working mother to twins made it difficult to fulfill her duties to Mr. Kane's satisfaction, especially when the managing Executive Assistant, Charlene Childress, hated her. Howard fought for her, but the other two partners voted him down.

She wished she was still in Illinois. She'd loved working for Sam Davis. He was a great boss. But she couldn't face him now.

She'd slept with Mike. She hadn't intended it to happen, but it had happened. And she'd gotten pregnant. She had no doubt that Mike would have been happy. Unfortunately, she'd taken the pregnancy test on the morning of his funeral. Watching Sam and his family that day mourn the loss of his son, she couldn't bring herself to tell them. And then her aunt had died, and, as Mike had promised, she'd left the house in Colonial Beach to Mary. Mary had taken leave to deal with the infighting among her cousins, her aunt's kids, over the will. It took months. Meanwhile, Mary gave birth to the twins in Virginia. She returned to Illinois only to find Sam and his family preoccupied by an attack on his daughter, Miranda, and then her engagement to Mike's best friend, Dan Bradley. Mary'd lost her nerve and moved back to Virginia.

She'd tried living in her house in Colonial Beach, only to discover jobs were in short supply. She'd been able to get an interview with Mr. Fox because Sam had recommended her. But it was too far for her to commute to Arlington. She'd never see her babies. So, she'd found an apartment and allowed her cousin Esmie to live in the house.

She couldn't send the twins to daycare today. Thank God for Max. Maxine James was her best friend. Max lived off her trust fund. She had agreed to watch the twins today so Mary wouldn't have to take leave on her new boss's first day...at a price. But she couldn't rely on Max all the time. She was going to have to find a better solution...like a nanny. She just didn't know how she'd ever afford it.

For whatever reason, Max had started pushing for Mary to go out with Chaz Petersen again. Chaz was a twice-divorced frat boy she'd gone out with once in college. They'd gone to school together since kindergarten. Max had set them up on the blind date. Mary had told her then she'd never liked Chaz. He was a narcissist. Max had dropped it back then, but recently, she'd started pushing him as a great catch, perhaps because she was on again with her on-again-off-again college love, Rob Hanson. Mary had to agree to consider a double date to get her help this time. Blech, she thought.

She sighed heavily and pulled her long, dark hair up in a

sloppy bun. She applied some concealer under her eyes and put on some lipstick. She still looked tired, but she could manage. She slipped her blazer over her blouse and stepped into her shoes. She slung her purse over her shoulder and headed out the door.

******

Declan stood patiently waiting in the line. The woman in front of him smiled pleasantly at him. "The lines are so long this time of the morning. All of this for a cup of coffee," she giggled.

"Aye, 'tis inconvenient at dat, but I'm needin' da caffeine dis mornin'. Jet lag," he winked.

The woman looked lovestruck. "Oh, what a lovely accent. Where are you from?"

He smiled. Yanks were all about the accent. "Ireland. But I live in London at da present moment."

"Ireland? Really?" the woman gushed.

"Aye, would ye like me to sing *Danny Boy* fer ye to prove it?" he smiled. She wasn't bad looking. She had a nice figure. And she was pleasant.

"Sherry!" came a man's voice from the door. "What's taking so long?"

The woman's face fell, and Declan took a half step back. Sherry was not available. She wasn't so very good-looking. He had no desire to fight anyone.

He smoothed down his lapel on his suit jacket and looked at the wall. Sherry's boyfriend stomped toward her.

"I'm in line. What do you want? I have to wait my turn," she retorted, rolling her eyes and tossing her hair. The boyfriend scowled and looked Declan up and down. Declan smiled and nodded to him.

Somewhere near the front of the line, a child began to cry. The child's mother pleaded for her to stop making a fuss. She wanted a cookie, but the mother told her she only had enough for what she'd ordered and that she could have a cookie when they got home.

"You talkin' to my girl?" the boyfriend grumbled.

"We exchanged pleasantries," Declan said.

"What does that mean?" the boyfriend blustered.

Declan was dumbfounded. "Um, dat we said hello te each other," he said.

"What are ya? English?" the boyfriend demanded.

"Lord, no. Irish."

"Do you think you're Prince Harry or somethin'?" the boyfriend continued.

"Again, no. Because I'm Irish," Declan retorted with a smile that only seemed to infuriate Sherry's boyfriend.

From the front of the line, Declan heard a harried-looking young woman say, "Pick up for Fox, Goodwin, and Kane." Then she handed a cookie to the child's mother and said, "For your daughter." His heart skipped a beat. It was an odd sensation. He wasn't sure what to make of it.

"Excuse me, dat's my colleague. I'll be leavin' ye," he said with a bow, thanking God for an easy escape. He wasn't afraid of the boyfriend, but he had no desire to get into an altercation over a simple flirtation. "Pardon me, Miss. I'm Declan Mahoney from Jude Rollins, Barristers. I'm joinin' yer firm dis mornin'. Let me get da bill and help carry it."

The woman turned to look at him. He was dumbstruck again. She put Sherry to shame. She was a rare beauty with long dark brown hair, big soulful brown eyes framed in long doe-like lashes, with a pert nose, and a mouth he immediately longed to kiss. He blinked and regained his senses before smiling pleasantly and hopefully not lecherously.

"Oh, thank you, Mr. Mahoney. Good morning. I don't mind, really." On second glance, she looked tired, but she was still undeniably pretty. Her dark brown hair was pulled up in a sloppy bun. He shook her hand.

He felt like he'd been hit by lightning. "Pure feek," he mumbled. "And yer name, Miss?" he asked cordially.

"M...Mary Cummings. I'm your executive assistant," she stammered.

"Well den, Mary Cummings, I insist." He paid for the coffees, and he was glad he did and that he'd offered to help carry them because the barista piled 34 different to-go coffees on the counter. He grabbed half. Why on earth had this woman tried to get this order by herself?

CHAPTER 2

Declan and Mary had no sooner exited the elevator on the floor to the offices of Fox Goodwin and Kane when a woman accosted poor Mary.

"Where have you been? Your new boss will be here any minute, and you're dawdling at the coffee shop next door, flirting with strange men? Why would you bring someone up here? Do you want to be fired?" the nasty wench scolded his new assistant.

Declan set the coffees down on the receptionist's desk and turned to the woman. "Woah, who are ye, and why do ye think ye kin talk to her like dat?"

"None of your business. She never should have let you come up here."

"Agin, who are ye? I'm Declan Mahoney. And dis is where I'm supposed to be. I'm not so certain about ye," he said sternly.

"I don't care who...Declan Mahoney?" the mad woman barked.

"Aye. And ye?" he asked with authority.

"My apologies, Mister Mahoney. I thought you'd be... older. I'm Charlene Childress, Managing Executive Assistant. Mary has a problem getting to work on time. I was just reminding her that she needs to be punctual today," she smiled, holding out her hand to shake his.

He just looked at it and frowned. "Why? She's here at ten 'til, clearly before time, so dere's no reason te remind her te be punctual when she already is. Now is dere? As fer her flirtin', she was nuthin' but polite and professional when I introduced maself, unlike ye. Ye've offered me yer apologies, which are surely warranted, but ye owe her a few as well, now don't ye?"

He leaned back against the desk, crossed his feet at the ankles, and crossed his arms across his chest.

Mary snorted. It made him smile. It was true; she hadn't flirted. But he wouldn't have minded if she had. Mary was a cutie with a good personality, unlike this sour, wicked witch of the west. It gave him great pleasure to put Charlene Childress in her place.

"My apologies, Mary," she said after several long seconds under Declan's cold gaze.

"Thank you, Charlene. Coffee?" Mary said, smugly.

Declan smiled again. "Now, which way to my office, Miss Cummings?" he asked, addressing Mary directly so as to cut off any chance of Charlene's offering assistance.

"Um, yes. Right this way, Mr. Mahoney. I've unpacked your boxes as per your instructions, and IT has set up your computer already, so you should be all set up for business," she said, walking just in front of him down a cherrywood wainscoted hallway with marble-tiled flooring. Her heels clicked on the tiles, but she moved gracefully and confidently. Charlene may have assigned Mary to him as a punishment, but he was happy that she had. He liked Mary immediately, almost as fast as he'd disliked Charlene.

At the end of the hallway, Mary pointed to a cherrywood door. "My desk is just over there," she said, pointing around the corner to an open space filled with cubicles. "The one closest to your office. If you need me, just press the intercom. It connects to my line."

She smiled and clasped her hands behind her back, swaying like a child.

"As ye walked me te my office, allow me te walk ye te yers," he said, grinning. Uh-oh, he thought. She was really cute. Really, really cute.

She nodded and walked toward the cubicles. It was only a

few short steps. He peered into her workspace as she deposited her purse into a desk drawer and took a seat. There must have been twenty pictures of two little red-headed toddlers. No pictures of a husband, though, he noted.

"Ye have children, do ye?" he asked, nodding at the largest picture. Children...He felt a pang of disappointment. Especially little children were his kryptonite. He liked them well enough, but he was a complete buffoon around them.

"Oh, yes. Dani and Randy. Fraternal twins. They're almost three."

"And dere dad, what does he do?" Declan asked, trying to sound casual. He died, he thought.

"He died before they were born," she said sadly. How had he known? He was baffled.

"Oh, I'm so sorry, I shouldna 'ave pried," he replied.

"No, it's okay. Most people are curious," she smiled again.

He nodded and pointed at his office door, turned, and walked back to it, opening it and stepping inside his own workspace. He closed the door behind him. He smiled to himself. Alright then, he thought. He wouldn't cross any lines, but he wasn't going to let anyone hurt that girl. Something was telling him he needed to watch over her. It felt almost like a familial obligation.

He felt a breeze blow gently across his shoulder and looked around for the source as the air conditioning kicked on.

He walked over to his desk and took a seat behind the massive piece of furniture. He opened the laptop and was greeted immediately with a video chat invitation. He clicked on it. "Aye, Gavin, me lad, 'ello. How are ye? I was sorry te hear of your abuelo's passin'," he said to the image of his cousin on the screen.

"I'm alright, Declan. Thanks. I'm about to board a plane to Reagan. I've got some business in DC tomorrow, but I have some time today if you'd like to meet for lunch."

"Aye, I can manage dat. Do ye need a car te pick ye up? I can get the firm to send one over fer ye?"

Gavin grinned and laughed. "Nah, I have a car and driver arranged."

"Oh, dat's right, you're a robber baron, aren't ye? Ye can buy lunch. I'll get my pretty assistant te get us reservations at da best and most expensive restaurant. I'll forward ye da details," Declan teased.

"Sure, but remember there are sexual harassment laws in this country. Your pretty assistant should be referred to just as your assistant," Gavin said with a wink. "See you in a few hours."

Declan disconnected the video call and hit the intercom on his desk phone. "Miss Cummings, I need lunch reservations fer maself and ma American cousin today. Make it at the most expensive place ye kin; he's payin'," he said.

"Um, yes sir…under your name?" Mary's voice came back over the speaker.

"Aye, dat's fine. Just forward me da information, and I'll git it te him. Thank ye. And did we git dat meetin' set up wid Sabah at da Smithsonian?"

"Yes, tomorrow at 2:30."

CHAPTER 3

Mary spent the morning researching the items on the list of artifacts the Grand Egyptian was requesting to help prepare the brief they'd need. It was just preliminary work. She'd hand the information over to Mr. Mahoney, and he'd prepare the brief, but she was totally engrossed. It was the most interesting work she'd done in a long while.

She started with a portion of papyrus uncovered in a labor supervisor's tomb in Giza. It appeared to be a portion of a ledger of sorts outlining supplies required for a portion of the construction of the Great Pyramid and appeared to include a stipend for wages along with the number of laborers required to complete the project. It could be clear proof that the laborers were skilled and valued...and not slaves.

Mary was deep into her research when Charlene dropped a stack of files on her desk. "Mr. Fox needs these briefs completed today," she announced smugly.

Mary looked at the stack in dismay as a masculine but elegant hand picked up the files and shoved them into Charlene's arms. "Then, one of Mr. Fox's assistants should git te work on dem. Miss Cummings is busy...and ma assistant," Declan said.

"She's paid by this firm," Charlene protested.

"Perhaps ye should check the terms of my contract. I require a dedicated Executive Assistant. Dat means she works exclusively on ma project, and ye can take yer files and shove dem," he said, stepping closer, forcing her to back up.

"I...uh...I need her to do these. Nobody else is available."

"Do it yerself den. She's not available either," he commanded.

Mary looked away and smiled.

Charlene stomped off. He smiled at Mary. "Go take yer lunch now. I'm headin' out te meet ma cousin. We have notes te go over dis afternoon fer da meetin' tomorrow. Don't let her give ye any extra tasks. Ye have enough work of yer own," he said, tapping the top of the cubicle partition with his fist to accentuate his point.

God, he was good-looking. He stood about 5'11" tall, with dark curly hair and steel blue eyes. He was fit. He knew how to wear a suit. He had a dazzling smile. Oddly, he reminded her of someone, but she couldn't put a finger on who. Mary swallowed hard and tried not to stare at him as he walked away. Howard Fox emerged from his office and hurried to catch up to Declan. She waited until she heard the elevator doors open and close from down the hallway before she opened her desk drawer, took out her purse, and made her way to the elevators herself.

Mary made her way to a small café a few blocks down from the office. As she walked, she took out her phone to call Max and check on the kids.

Max picked up on the third ring. "Hi, Mama. How's the new boss?" Max asked cheerfully.

"Oh, Max, he's amazing. He's put Charlene in her place several times today already, and the work is really interesting. Oh, and he has this amazing accent."

"OMG! You like him!" Max squealed.

"Don't be silly. He's my boss. But I will admit he's not hard to look at," Mary giggled.

"How old is he? I pictured some old man," Max retorted.

"I know. Right? But no. He's probably in his mid-thirties. He reminds me of someone. I just can't figure out who," she said with a smile. "Anyway, how are the kiddos? Randy feeling any better?"

"Fever's all gone, and he's back to his wild man status,"

Max laughed.

"How's Dani? Any symptoms?"

"Not that I've noticed," Max assured her.

Mary pushed open the door to the café and made her way to the counter. "I'm about to grab some lunch, Max. I'll check in again later. Thanks again for today," she said, getting in the line behind the mailroom kid from her office.

"No problem, Babe. I got your back. Plus, you promised to go out with Rob and me…so you're tops in my book. Rob really wants to get Chaz a good girl to help him settle down. Enjoy your lunch."

Mary rolled her eyes and disconnected just as it was her turn to order. "Hi. I'll have the chicken salad on the croissant and a cup of chicken noodle soup with a sweetened iced tea. Thank you."

"$18.84," said the cashier.

Mary handed over a twenty-dollar bill and dug out two ones, handing them over as well. "Keep the change. Thanks."

She turned to see Wade Hinson, a first-year attorney fresh out of law school, and Gail Jacobs, a clerical assistant, snuggled cozily down in a corner of the restaurant. They were trying to be discreet, she knew, but my God, they were failing miserably. Everyone knew. She smiled and looked the other way. Let them have their illusion. It wasn't hurting anyone.

She took her food and found a table near the door. No sooner had she unpacked her bag and taken a bite of her sandwich than Charlene stood over her. "Mr. Kane is displeased with your refusal to do the work I assigned you. You can expect to be written up when you get back from lunch," she laughed mirthlessly.

Mary sighed. "And you can expect Mr. Mahoney to dispute it. I get the impression he isn't the kind of man you want to mess with, Charlene, but you go right ahead and try. I think he enjoys knocking you down a few pegs."

******

Declan grasped his cousin's hand. "Gavin, ma lad. Good te see ye. Ye look well."

"You, too, Declan," Gavin said, standing to shake hands. "How're Grand Da and Nan?"

"They're doin' well. I hear ye got married and have a baby garl of yer own," Declan continued, taking a seat.

"Not just a baby girl. It turns out Shannon had a son she never bothered to tell me about. His name is Hal, and he looks just like me. He's 7. Here. This is Hal. This is Jason, my stepson, and this is Estrella Moira," Gavin told him, swiping through pictures on his phone. "And, mi Vida, DeBella." The picture was of a gorgeous blonde. Gavin had never had a problem with women. He could smile, and they'd throw themselves at his feet. Declan wasn't surprised that his wife was stunningly beautiful.

"Ye have a lovely family," Declan said. Then, swiping back to the picture of Hal, he chuckled at the resemblance between Gavin and his son. "He looks just like ye at dat age. How'd ye come te find out about him?"

Gavin sighed. "Shannon figured out about Abuelo and decided to sue me for child support. Also, there was a school bus hijacking with a bomb on the bus. We got all the kids off safely. I was working for the Fredericksburg PD at the time. Anyway, his name appeared on the roster, but he hadn't been on the bus that day. I put it together when I saw his name...Henry James... Gibbons at that time. It's been changed to Mahoney since then."

"Really? What 'appened wid da school bus?" Declan asked coolly.

"The hijackers were trying to kill Hal. Back in Afghanistan, a kid got killed from back home. His parents blamed me and wanted me to experience what they had gone through. Shannon was killed. I got wounded. It was a terrible ordeal. But Hal's safe and loved now."

"Dat's...odd. Dere was a school bus hijacking on my street in Dublin in November...Dere was a bomb on da bus," Declan mused. The two of them looked at each other in silence until the waiter appeared to take their order. Declan wondered how much Gavin really knew. He had a feeling it was more than he was letting on. He shook off the feeling. "She figured out who yer Abuelo was, hey? Gran Da escaped her scrutiny?"

"Apparently. She never mentioned him."

Declan laughed. "And neither did ye," he guffawed.

The cousins had a pleasant meal. As the waiter retrieved the check, Gavin excused himself to go to the men's room. Declan looked up to see a uniformed army officer standing over him. "Hello?" he said.

"Declan Mahoney?" the officer asked.

"Aye, and who are ye?"

"Captain Gil Talbert, Sir. I was told to deliver this to you," he said mysteriously.

"What is it?" Declan asked, taking the manilla envelope.

"No idea, Mr. Mahoney. I'm just a courier. All I know is that a high-ranking officer with CID sent it."

Declan looked at the envelope. He didn't know any high-ranking officers in CID.

When he looked up again, Captain Talbert was gone.

Gavin returned and sat back down. "What's that?" he asked, seeing the envelope.

"No idea. Let's see," Declan said, smiling. He opened the envelope and pulled out a document. "Well, it appears te be a dossier on Dr. Sabah Al-Maghrabi. I have a meeting with her tomorrow."

"Weird. Where did it come from?"

"Some Army officer with CID handed it te me," Declan mused.

Gavin chuckled. "Are you some kind of spy, Dec?"

"Ha. I'm a boring barrister who works with boring old artifacts," Declan retorted.

"Sure, ya are," Gavin teased.

"And ye? Not only are ye a man of business now, ye've inherited a treasure trove from yer wife's uncail, I hear," Declan said, winking. "Dat's why yer buyin'."

Gavin laughed. "I swear if I'd have known he had so much money and stuff, I'd have said no when he asked me to be the executor of his will. Plus, I had no idea his way of fairly dividing his personal property was to leave it to me and let me decide what to do with it. Bob was a bit of a character. But I loved the old guy."

CHAPTER 4

Sabah Al-Maghrabi was more than she seemed. Her father was Egyptian, and her mother was an ex-patriot from England. She had deep connections to the Muslim Brotherhood, her father and uncles all being members. She was engaged to the son of a Russian banking oligarch. The bank had ties to the Muslim Brotherhood through several Brotherhood member-owned businesses. The bank appeared to launder money for the Brotherhood as well.

Declan briefly considered removing Mary from his team but determined it was already too late for that course of action. She'd been the one to arrange the meeting. She was already known to Sabah. Plus, there was the secret Howard had revealed to him. He'd be better able to keep her safe if he kept her close.

He drummed his fingers on his desk. He wracked his brain, but he couldn't figure out who was helping him in CID. It didn't surprise him that CID had an eye on this project. He'd long suspected the Brotherhood had a foothold in the Grand Egyptian Museum. It only made sense that CID would be aware of this and would want to keep an eye on it, but who would know his interest in this situation and give him a head's up? He took out his phone and texted his one true friend, "Who do you know in CID?"

"No one you don't know," came the cryptic reply.

He looked at the framed photo of his grandparents on his desk and wondered briefly if his Grand Da knew and had a hand in this, but he was fairly certain Grand Da didn't know he was more than a barrister. Grand Da was still prouder of Gavin than of Declan because of that Silver Star. If he had any idea of what Declan really was, Gavin wouldn't be the favorite.

He chuckled at his own jealousy and told himself that it wasn't Gavin's fault. It was just the way it was. Gavin was a good guy. He had earned that Silver Star, and he never lorded it over anyone. Declan liked Gavin. He just wished sometimes Grand Da valued him as much as he valued his American cousin. It was hard to compete with Captain America. And it all became crystal clear to him. "Son of a..." he said to the room.

"Have you met my cousin?" he texted again.

"No. But I know of him," came the reply.

His thoughts turned back to Mary when he heard the ruckus outside his office. Mr. Kane's raised voice was bellowing, "Miss Cummings, you've already been given a second chance! How do you think you're in any position to tell Mrs. Childress you won't do the work she assigns you? Please report to HR!"

Declan slammed his fist on the desk and stood. He flung open the door and strode out and over to the partner and Ms. Childress, who had ambushed poor Mary in her cubicle.

"She'll not be doin' any such thing. She did'na refuse da work. I told Mrs. Childress she would'na be doin' any work aside from ma project per ma contract wid yer firm. I assure ye, I intend to enforce dat clause. I require a dedicated Executive Assistant, exclusively mine. She will na suffer a reprimand at yer hand fer followin' my instruction, Mr. Kane."

Mr. Kane looked like he might explode, but he turned to face Declan. "Mrs. Childress tells me that the files were yours," he said through gritted teeth. He was trying to tell Declan something, Declan thought.

"I assure ye, it was na," Declan said, crossing his arms again with a steely stare. "Miss Cummings is doin' the work I assigned her. I never asked, nor do I need her to, work on Howard Fox's briefs."

"Howard's briefs?" He turned to look at Charlene, who blushed.

"You misunderstood me, Mr. Kane. The files were not Mr. Mahoney's project, but she's still my subordinate. I needed her to work on them."

Mr. Kane shook his head. "My apologies, Mary. Mr. Mahoney is correct. You are assigned exclusively to his project. Mrs. Childress, I told you to refrain from assigning her work that does not come from Mr. Mahoney," Mr. Kane acquiesced. Declan could see that the man was livid. Good. He should be. "Pack up. You're fired. Security will see you out."

"But Mr. Kane...I've been here for ten years," Charlene argued.

"All the more reason...Charlene, I can't believe you are this petty," Mr. Kane said, turning and walking away.

Fifteen minutes later, Charlene was escorted out by security. Declan stood beside Mary and watched her go. "Mr. Mahoney," Mary whispered.

"Hmmm?" he replied.

"This has been an awesome day," she snickered. Mary was adorable. His heart nearly burst looking at her.

He smiled and made a decision. The Muslim Brotherhood would never even come close to her.

CHAPTER 5

Mary pushed Dani on the swing while Max pushed Randy. "So, she really got fired?" Max laughed. "Oh my God, that's so great! Tell me more about *him.*"

"There's nothing much to tell," Mary said, blushing. "He's smart…I mean super smart…like Mike was. And he doesn't take crap off anyone. Oh, and he has the sexiest accent. I mean, I thought an English accent was sexy, but Irish is…sexier. He's really fit. You can tell he's cut, even through the suit. He has the nicest smile. And, OMG, his eyes are this steely blue. With all that dark curly hair, he's quite good-looking. But he's kind, too. He's a bit of a flirt. But he gets away with it because he's just so damned charming," Mary gushed.

"Nothing much to tell…except you are totally crushing on him!" Max teased. She laughed. Mary rolled her eyes.

"He stood up for me, Max. I'm grateful. But our relationship is completely professional," she insisted. But was it? She certainly couldn't deny she found him attractive. Beyond that, though, she felt drawn to him.

They took the twins for ice cream and walked back to Mary's apartment building with the twins in their double stroller. They stopped, and Mary tried to wipe away some of the sticky from her son's face with a wipe.

"Oh, look, someone's moving into the apartment next to you, Mare. Odd time of the day for it," Max observed. Sure enough, a moving truck had pulled in, and movers were bringing new furniture into the apartment next to hers. The new neighbor got out of a Mercedes and strode toward the apartment. Mary grabbed Max's arm.

"Holy cow! That's *him*!" she exclaimed.

"Him?" Max asked.

"Mr. Mahoney," Mary said. How was he here? How was he her neighbor? Mary didn't know what to think.

A few hours later, she gave into her curiosity, and having the kids down for the night, and baby monitor in hand, she knocked on his door with a bottle of wine as a welcome gift.

"One moment," he called from inside the apartment. He opened the door and looked shocked to see his assistant. "Miss Cummings?" he asked, looking around to see if there was anyone with her. "What are ye doin' here?"

"I live here," she said.

"Ye live here?" he asked, clearly perplexed as he was standing in his own apartment.

"Oh, no. There," she laughed, pointing to her apartment next door.

He looked where she pointed. "Ye're kiddin? That's quite a coincidence! What a nice surprise!" he said with a smile. "Would ye like to come in? I'm just puttin' together ma sound system."

"Oh, no. I can't. I just brought you this bottle of wine to say welcome to the building, but my kids are in bed..." she explained.

"Thank ye. I don't have any glasses unpacked yet, but I'd love to share a glass wid ye," he hinted.

"Oh, sure. Come on over," she smiled, happily taking the bait.

He grabbed his keys from a table beside the door, closed the door behind him, and motioned for her to lead the way. She opened her own door and invited him to have a seat.

"Pardon the mess. My kids were home sick today. My best friend, Max...Maxine...watched them. She has the luxury of being wealthy," she exclaimed.

"It's just a few toys," he smiled. "It's nice te see a home

dat's lived in. Ma sister has chisellers. Well, two of dem do, actually, though I've never met Roana's son. Dat's a story fer another time. A little messy. It's da way it's supposed te be." He picked up a stuffy puppy with floppy ears and twisted it so that the ears flopped.

Mary walked into her kitchen. Once out of his sightline, she took a deep breath and exhaled nervously. He was so good-looking…and sitting on her sofa. She grabbed two wine glasses from her cabinet and a corkscrew from a drawer. She put some grapes, cheese, and crackers on a serving platter. She checked her teeth in the reflection of her oven door, took another cleansing breath, and adjusted her cleavage. She straightened her spine, grabbed the items she'd gathered, and headed back to the living room.

He stood as she entered. What a gentleman, she thought. God, he really reminded her of someone. She handed him the corkscrew and put the glasses and food down on the coffee table.

"So," she said, sitting on the sofa, "how is it my new boss is also my new neighbor?"

"Oh, I hate hotels. I generally get an apartment when working on a project such as dis. It's more comfortable…and cheaper, even buyin' new furniture," he replied, flashing a flirtatious smile. Mary's heart fluttered. Just so damned good-looking, she thought.

"What do you do with it when you're done?" she asked, laughing.

"I usually donate it te Saint Vincent De Paul," he answered. "It is odd dat I should 'ave chosen an apartment next to ye, Miss Cummings. I hope it isn't too much of an imposition te ye. If ye aren't comfortable wid it, I can move next month." He opened the wine with a pop and poured out two glasses.

"Oh, don't do that, Mr. Mahoney. It's fine," she said, taking a sip of the wine.

"In dat case, kin you do me da favor of callin' me Declan?"

She smiled brightly. "I can do that, Declan. And I'm just Mary."

"Ye aren't 'jest' anything, Mary. Ye're extraordinary. Don't let anybody tell ye otherwise," he offered. She felt the flush in her cheeks and looked away from his gaze.

They sat and chatted as they drank the wine. He told her that he had three sisters, one two years his junior whom he hadn't seen in five years after she eloped, one happily married with six children in Dublin still, and one just 15 years old. He told her about Dublin. She told him how her grandfather had been from Ireland, and she had been once after he had died. She agreed it was a beautiful country. She told him about Mike, who she rarely ever talked about. He expressed his sympathies over her loss. They finished the bottle.

He admired her old beat-up guitar, sitting in the corner. She asked if he played. He acknowledged he did play a little. She handed it over to him, and he started playing a song she'd never heard. He sang along about "young William McBride's" grave, who died in 1916. She listened, completely enraptured. She asked the name of the song. He told her *Green Fields of France*. He asked her to play something. She played "The Boxer." Poorly, she thought, and he applauded her effort.

At 10:26, her phone rang. "Hello, Max," she said, answering the call. "No, I wasn't in bed yet. It's fine – I haven't seen it. – Where do you think you left it?" Declan gave her a quizzical look. "My friend lost her bracelet. It was a gift from her dad. A gold bangle." He looked around and stuck his hands in between the couch cushions, pulling out a gold bangle. "Oh! Yay! Declan found it, Max. It fell between the couch cushions. – Yes. — Don't be crude. He's my boss. I took him a bottle of wine as a welcome gift, and we drank a few glasses, is all. – Max! OMG!"

He laughed good naturedly and checked his watch. "Oh,

look at da time. I'll be leavin' now. I'd be happy te have ye ride wid me to work in da mornin'. We're goin' to da same place after all."

"I couldn't. I have to take the kids to daycare and pick them up," Mary protested.

"I do na mind. Really. 7 am?" he insisted.

"Their car seats…" she said.

"Den, we'll take yer car, and I'll git two car seats tomorrow evenin'," Declan said with a smile, rising and moving toward the door. "Goodnight, Mary. I'll see ye in da mornin'. And goodnight te ye, Max." Then he was gone.

CHAPTER 6

Declan stood by Mary's car, waiting for her. He saw the man first, but he purposely did not react. Instead, he unbuttoned his suit jacket and adjusted his shoulder holster, revealing the weapon hidden under his jacket. He rebuttoned the jacket, and the man had gone.

Moments later, Mary emerged from her apartment with a chubby child on each hip. He smiled, waved, and moved toward her. "Kin I help ye?" he asked. "I would na want to scare da chisellers." But the boy, Randy, reached for him immediately.

Mary laughed as he took her son from her. "Luckily, he's obsessed with men lately," she said.

"Ye should be more careful, Little Man, but thankfully, I'm a nice guy," he laughed as the boy looked him directly in the eyes. "Ye know, ye look like my Uncail Daithi…red hair and violet eyes. But dat's a good thing. He's a good-lookin' man, he is."

"Ewes tawk funty," the boy giggled.

"Aye, dat I do," Declan chuckled. He was feckin' nervous. Kids made him nervous. He was babbling. Shut up, eegit, he thought.

They dropped the twins off at daycare, and Mary drove through McDonald's drive-thru.

"I'm not getting the coffee today. I just do it on Mondays," she explained.

They pulled into the parking garage, and he told her to park in his space. She did as he said. Charlene was beside her car before she even got out. "How dare you!" screamed the crazy woman. Declan had to pull her off Mary.

"What da hell!" he yelled, pushing her away.

"She's sleeping with you!" Charlene accused.

"News ta me," he replied. "We live in da same buildin'. We shared a ride. Not that we owe ye an explanation, Ye, however, have been fired, and ye have no business here. So, Mary'll be callin' da police now, and since we're right under a CCTV camera, you'll be charged wid assault and battery."

Mary took out her phone and called 911.

"I'm not going anywhere! I'm going to stand right here and tell everyone how you two are sleeping together."

He sighed. "Go ahead. See if it changes anything. I still like her and think ye're a ragin' focloir.ie. Dat's bitch in yer vernacular."

Mary grabbed Declan's arm. "Let's just go, Declan. I don't care what she does."

He turned and looked at Mary. "Alright, den. We have a meetin' dis afternoon. I need dat research. We'll wait fer da police upstairs."

She smiled and took his hand. It was the strangest sensation. He'd never felt anything like it. It was a happy feeling. God, had he been unhappy? She was a single mother. She was his assistant. She should be off-limits. She was off-limits. What was he thinking?

He smiled and raised her hand to his mouth, kissing her fingertips. He clasped her hand in his, and they headed to the elevator. He expected her to drop his hand when the doors closed. She didn't. He grinned.

When they reached his office door, she stood on tip-toe and kissed his cheek before letting go of his hand and walking to her cubicle. He heard a few whispered comments. Her back stiffened. She set her purse on her desk and walked out to the center of the room, and said loudly, "I've more regrets in my life than I care to numerate. None of them are for things I did.

Only for things I was afraid to do. If you feel the need to gossip about me, just know I really don't give a damn what any of you think. I fell in love once, and I didn't act on it until it was too late. I like that man, and he seems to like me. I know the employee handbook inside out. There is no policy against dating. Good? Good."

He walked to her desk as she came back to it and took a seat. "What happened to 'he's my boss'?" he asked.

"I slept on it and decided screw it," she replied.

"Were you going to tell me?" he asked.

"You moved into an apartment next to me to be close to me. I figured you'd be okay with it. Am I wrong?" she asked. God, the way this girl flirted…

He smiled. "Ye're not."

"I have work to do," she said. He nodded and went back to his office.

"Mary's feckin' amazin'," he said to the breeze that he felt across his shoulder as the AC kicked on. "But whoever ye are, ye already know it, don't ye?"

That's when he heard the blood-curdling scream.

He ran out of his office to see everyone standing. George Goodwin and Roland Kane appeared outside their doors. Tiffany Fowler, a clerical assistant, stood outside Howard Fox's office door, screaming.

Tiffany was just a girl, really, an intern in an undergraduate program at James Madison University, barely 20. Declan ran toward her. He reached the door and saw the grizzly scene inside the office. "Oh, dear Lord!" he exclaimed. "Come away, Miss Fowler. Mary, call 911 again. Advise dem that dere's been a homicide. Nobody else touch dis door."

CHAPTER 7

The police brought Charlene up to the office. She was hysterical at this point. She pointed at Mary and Declan and shouted, "It was them! They killed Howard!"

"Impossible, Mrs. Childress. They were drinking a bottle of wine in Miss Cummings apartment at the time of death," Mr. Kane said.

"Your man was following Mary?" Declan asked, arms crossed.

"Yes, Declan. He is our man."

"What man?" Mary asked. They ignored her.

"Why did you have her followed?" Declan continued, holding up his hand.

"Howard was worried about her," Roland Kane continued.

"What man?" Mary asked again.

"Sherry's boyfriend," Declan said.

"Who?" Mary inquired.

"Sherry's boyfriend…from the coffee shop yesterday morning. He yelled at me for talking to Sherry," Declan explained.

"Someone is following me, and you didn't tell me?" Mary said, horrified.

Declan blushed. "Aye, I did na want te scare ye until I knew more. I'm sorry. Clearly, ye are not easily scared."

Mary shook her head and looked down. "That's not true. I am scared."

Declan smiled. Oddly, she wasn't angry. She was grateful. She'd only known him a day, but she had a feeling Mike approved.

No. She had more than a feeling.

She'd dreamed last night of Mike. He had played with the

twins. He'd hugged them both. He'd looked up at her, and he'd stood and walked toward her. He'd kissed her deeply. Then he'd said, "It's okay, Mary. I like him. He'll be there for you."

She'd asked who he meant.

"Declan, of course. I asked him to protect you. He said he would. Let him," Mike had said before fading, and she had awakened.

She took a step toward Declan and wrapped her arms around his neck. She appeared to catch him by surprise, but he put his hands on her waist. "I'm really sorry, Mary. I should 'ave told ye."

"I'm not a shrinking violet, Declan," she replied, hugging him.

"Obviously," he laughed.

The police took everyone's statements. Declan and Mary grabbed their laptops and headed down to the coffee shop to make use of the Wi-Fi. Grizzly murder or not, they still had to keep their appointment with Dr. Al-Maghrabi, and they needed the minimum of preparation.

Mary delved back into the historical importance of the Workman's Contract, as archaeologists named it, that was more of a ledger than a contract but was named thusly as it outlined salary for laborers. The artifact was a papyrus scroll, preserved in a clay jar, much like the Dead Sea Scrolls, uncovered in the tomb of a foreman in the workers' cemetery. The scroll was decayed so that it could not be opened, but the hieroglyphics had been deciphered with the assistance of technology created at the University of Kentucky to virtually unroll the scroll.

Declan researched the hieroglyphics and their translation per Egyptologists at various universities. The consensus was that the Workman's Contract outlined payment for work. There was some disagreement over minor wording.

Egypt desperately wanted this artifact back. Declan agreed

that it should belong to Egypt. Right now, it was in the possession of the Smithsonian, though not part of a display and apparently on loan from a private owner. It was, however, available to Egyptologists for study, which was why the Smithsonian was reticent to return it.

Declan had to admit it was hard to concentrate, what with the coffee shop bustling around them and the knowledge of what had happened next door. While Mary was no shrinking violet, as she had said, she was a human being with a kind heart. She suddenly broke down in tears.

He closed his laptop and pushed it away from him, moving his chair closer to hers. She laid her head on his shoulder and cried. He wrapped his arm around her, pulling her close to him. He kissed the top of her head. Then he rested his chin there. "I wish we could reschedule dis meetin', ma Lovely, but it can na be done. It's important te da client, but it doesn't have te be determined today. We have time te negotiate later. We'll just let dis be an introduction. Put away yer work. 'Tis enuff fer today," he said kindly.

"I'm sorry. It's just so awful," she wailed.

"Aye, dat it is. Dat it is," he agreed. He wished he had the words to comfort her. A downside to being him was an emotional disconnect from tragedy. If he didn't disconnect, he'd never be able to get out of bed. But looking at Mary, he started to feel. Honestly, it was a little scary. Being unaccustomed to feeling, he had no words. So, he just let her cry as he held her.

Charlene pushed her way into the coffee shop. She stomped over to where Mary clung to Declan. "It's all your fault…if you'd only done what I asked…" she hissed.

"It is na her job. You should 'ave done it yerself if it was so important," Declan retorted.

"I couldn't assign it to anyone else and put them in danger, too." Charlene cried. Had she demoted Mary to protect her? Declan wasn't certain. He doubted it, but that was what she seemed to be implying.

"Whereas Mary already was in danger despite yer efforts te protect her?" he said. She nodded and smiled uncontrollably, revealing her motives were not as she had suggested. "What's in da files, Charlene?"

She started to shake. "I really don't know. I only know Howard was terrified," she laughed.

Declan looked at Mary. "I don't know, Declan. I only got a glimpse. There were three files. One was a tax issue for an American actress who took a commercial in Egypt. The second was a corporation setting up offices in Cairo. And the third was a student traveling in Egypt who was arrested for petty theft at the gift shop in Giza," Mary explained.

"Dey were all in Egypt?" he asked. Mary nodded. "Damn," he said.

"What?"

"Nuthin'. We have a meetin'. Let's go," he said.

Charlene stomped her foot. She reached out to grab Mary. Declan intercepted her arm. "Do na touch her," he said through gritted teeth. He flung her arm back, picked up his briefcase, and led Mary out of the coffee shop. Outside, he hailed a cab. They climbed into the back, and the cab pulled away.

******

Charlene had put a target on Mary. He was sure of it. But without more information, he couldn't be certain who was coming after her or why. He'd followed breadcrumbs here after the bus hijacking in November. But he hadn't even gotten the information from Howard yet, and Howard was gone.

They rode in silence. On the other side of the Arlington Memorial Bridge, they made their way past the International Spy Museum. Declan chuckled as they drove past. They arrived at the West Wing Café moments later.

Sabah Al-Maghrabi was waiting for them at a table by the window. She was an attractive woman in her mid-thirties. She looked nervous, Declan thought. They had only just walked through the door when a bullet pierced the window and struck Sabah in the head. Declan turned to see the telltale red dot on Mary's head. He slammed her to the ground just before the second bullet pierced the glass door behind them. Mary screamed as he covered her with his own body.

In the confusion that broke out with the shots, Declan grabbed Mary's hand, pulled her to standing, and ran, pulling her with him.

He ran back to the International Spy Museum, finding the back entrance he knew would be there. He shoved the keycard he had into the lock and slipped with Mary inside the building. He knew that the entrance they used was out of the view of the CCTV. He closed his eyes and pictured the museum's layout. They had entered an unmarked entrance with his key card. That would alert the US contact who had steered him to the law firm to begin with. And he had an idea who that was. They were in as safe a place as they could be for the moment.

They were in a corridor. The floor was linoleum. The walls were a light gray. There were no doors along the walls, just a long corridor that led to a single door that had a biometric scanner to access it.

Mary was still screaming. He grabbed her by both shoulders and gave her a gentle shake.

"Stop! Ye're safe fer da moment!" he exclaimed.

She looked at him and then at her surroundings, seeming to realize for the first time that he had pulled her away from the restaurant. She swallowed hard and flung herself into his arms before she started crying.

"My kids!" she exclaimed. She was overwhelmed with fear.

Declan heaved a sigh. "Call Max. Tell her to take da children to your family. If dey haven't run a background check on ye yet, they'll let her leave wid dem without followin' her. Hopefully, by da time dey do, they'll na know where dey went."

She reached for her phone. He grabbed her hand. "Ye'll have to wait until we go through dat door. Dere won't be a signal in dis hallway." She looked at her phone and nodded.

"How do we get past that scanner?" she asked.

"We have faith that the person who gave me da keycard also put my biometrics in da system," he said with a smile. He pushed her forward quickly, and when they reached the end of the hallway, he placed his hand on the scanner. As he suspected, access was granted. They went through the door and found themselves in the main hall of the museum.

Mary made the call. Max assured them she was leaving immediately. He quickly texted his friend, "Follow Max James. Make sure she gets the children she's transporting to Colonial Beach safely and without being followed."

"Who are they?" came the return text.

"They're under my protection, and I can't get to them right now. Just do it," he texted back.

"Done," came the reply. "Do you need extraction?"

"No. CID contact will provide," he answered.

Then he texted his American cousin. "Used pass card. Thanks. Need extraction for secretary and myself."

"Anything else?" came the curt reply

"Safe house?" he texted.

An address on Rodney Lane in Fredericksburg, VA, appeared.

"I sent Captain Talbert. Get yourself and the secretary to the safe house. BTW, who is she?"

"No comment," he replied.

"Understood. As long as you're confident in her. Get to

the safe house. There's an Escalade on the corner at the light. Kit inside," the phone read.

He stared at it for a full minute. He threw caution to the wind. "Gavin, I knew it was you." he texted.

Two minutes passed. "I gathered when you texted me directly," came the reply.

"What's your rank?" he texted.

"Lt. General," came the response.

"You suck, Captain America," he texted, shaking his head and laughing.

"That's Lt. General America, Major. Get moving. I don't want a dead J2 officer on my watch, especially not my cousin. Go."

"Let's go, Mary. Leave yer laptop and yer cell. Dey kin be traced." She dropped both devices into the nearest trash can as they strolled casually past James Bond's gold Aston Martin, and they walked out the front door.

"What about yours?" Mary asked as the door closed behind them.

He smiled. "Dey're encrypted."

They walked along the sidewalk on L'Enfant Plaza toward Benjamin Banneker Park. At the first red light, a black Escalade sat at the intersection. As they approached, the driver quickly got out and walked away without shutting the door or looking at Declan and Mary.

"Get in da passenger side," Declan whispered, releasing her arm and getting into the driver's seat. She crossed quickly in front of the SUV, opened the passenger side door, and got in as the light turned green.

CHAPTER 8

"Who are you, really?" Mary asked as Declan drove south on I-95.

"Declan Mahoney. I promise dat's ma real name," he answered with a smile. Mary's heart did a quick flip-flop in her chest.

"Are you really an attorney?" she continued.

"I am. And I really work for da barrister in London. But I'm more dan dat, as ye've deduced already," he said cryptically.

She sat in the passenger seat, staring at him. "Well?" she said at last.

"I'm wid J2," he said.

"I don't know what that is," she lied.

He laughed. God, he had a great laugh.

"It's Irish Military Intelligence," he replied.

"So, you're James Bond...Sean Connery style?" she asked.

"Hmmm. Only I have all ma hair," he said with a wink. He turned on the radio. Taylor Swift's "Bad Blood," filled the cabin of the SUV.

"Am I going to die?" she asked.

"No," he said. "I promise."

"Who were you texting?" Mary continued. She knew he wouldn't tell her, but she needed to keep talking. If she stopped, the fear would win.

"I can na say," he replied.

"But you know? It wasn't some faceless handler you've never met. You were laughing, like with a friend," she said. She shocked him. Apparently, he hadn't expected her to be so observant.

"Very good, Mary. Yes, I know da agent, personally. He… and yes, 'tis a man…sent me a dossier on Sabah Al-Maghrabi. She's connected te da Muslim Brotherhood."

"You trust this man?" she asked, wringing her hands together in her lap.

"Aye, wid ma very life," he assured her.

She sat there quietly for a minute, but to combat the fear, she focused on what she knew about Declan. It was more than she'd expected after just 30 hours. He really was a lawyer. He was really from Dublin. He was Irish Military. He had an American cousin. His name was really Declan…Mahoney.

"Oh, damn it!" she exclaimed. "Gavin Mahoney."

He choked on the air. "Wh….what?" he sputtered.

"Who," she corrected. "He's who you remind me of… Oh, God! Please don't tell him I'm here…or that I have Dani and Randy!" she pleaded, grabbing his arm.

He looked at her with his mouth wide open, then back at the road, then back at her.

"Ye…ye know my cousin?" he asked.

"Yes. Well, not well. I've met him. He was a client of my last boss," she explained, a new fear filling her.

"And why do ye not want him to know about yer babies?" he asked. "Wait, Randy looks like ma uncail. Dey're na Gavin's are dey?"

"What? Oh no! Babies always look like older men. No. Their dad was Mike Davis. My boss's son. And I…kinda…never…told his family that I was pregnant," she admitted. "I meant to, but I just…chickened out. I have a letter. I just can't seem to mail it. And your cousin could tell them…and I could lose my babies. I just need to figure out how to tell them before the state trooper does it. He's kind of a Boy Scout. He'd never lie."

Declan burst out laughing. "Alright, Mary, I'll na tell him, but yer wrong about his not ever lyin'."

She was confused by this response. Gavin Mahoney struck her as a very honest man. He'd been in the Army and with the state police. She stared at the road. "Oh my God, Gavin's your CID contact," she said suddenly.

Declan shook his head. "Aye. And now It's yer turn to keep quiet, Mary."

"I won't tell a soul," she promised. "Which of you has the higher rank?" she teased, wiggling in her seat.

"He does," he said, sounding disgusted. "Captain America is a three-star general." Then he laughed. "Ye're a smart one, Mary. I think ye may know more than ye think ye do. We'll have to work on figurin' out what dat is after we pick up some clothes and groceries."

CHAPTER 9

They drove south against rush hour traffic for about an hour. Before they made it to Fredericksburg, Declan exited at Aquia. He found a Walmart. He parked out of view of the CCTV cameras. "There's a wig and sunglasses in da bag in da backseat. Put dem on," he instructed Mary, pulling off his suit jacket and tie.

He mussed his hair and removed his holster. "There's clothes in here, too," Mary said, digging through the bag.

"Aye, give me a shirt," he said, stripping off his clean white dress shirt. She handed him a plain gray tee shirt, her breath catching at the sight of his muscular torso. He had a tribal tattoo around the top of his right bicep. He pulled the tee shirt on over his head quickly.

"Levis?" she asked with a suggestive grin.

"Aye, but close yer eyes, ye minx," he teased back.

She closed her eyes and covered them with her hand, but she peeked through her fingers as he deftly worked his way out of his suit pants and into the jeans. Having fastened the button, he grabbed her hand that "covered" her eyes and said, "Like what ye see?"

She nodded. He smiled and kissed her. She found herself melting into the unexpected kiss. He released her, and she was breathless. "Change yer clothes," he ordered her.

He turned away as she did as he told her. He did not peek, and she didn't know if she was relieved or disappointed by that. He tossed their discarded clothing into the bag. He put his holster and the weapon on over the tee shirt.

"Shouldn't you hide the gun?" Mary asked, concerned.

"Virginia is an open carry state. Conceal carry requires

permits. I 'ave dem, but dey have ma name on dem. Dey won't even ask about da gun as long as dey see it, but dey might if it's hidden, and dey happen to see it," he explained.

"What are we buying?" she asked.

"Da necessities," he replied. "Clothes, underwear, socks, toothbrushes, toiletries, groceries...to last a week. Just da bare minimum. Also, hair dye. Ye're goin' blonde, ma Lovely."

"And you?" she asked.

"I'll grow out ma facial hair, but dey aren't lookin' fer me."

She nodded. "Okay, Declan. I'll trust you."

"Weddin' rings," he announced. "We'll need weddin' rings. Dis house is in a neighborhood. Dere may be some interaction wid neighbors, though as little as we can manage," he told her. She dug through the bag, pulling out two ring boxes.

"Looks like somebody already thought of that," she observed. She took the diamond solitaire and matching wedding band out of one box and slipped them onto her finger. He took the men's band and did the same.

"I do," she whispered under her breath.

"What?" he asked.

"Nothing," she said. She was overcome by a deep sadness. Mike, she thought, why'd you leave me? She closed her eyes and pictured him. The picture offered no solace. He'd been so sick. He'd been pale and gaunt, with dark circles under his eyes. Her heart broke all over again, and a tear rolled down her cheek.

"Are ye alright, Mary?" Declan asked. He sounded sincere. She wiped away the tear and nodded yet again.

"What do I call you?" she asked.

"Declan. And I'll call ye Mary. The closer we stick to da truth, da more believable it will be. But we'll be Declan and Mary O'Mally. Newlyweds. Whirlwind romance. We just met 2 weeks ago in Cancun. It will help hide what we do na know about each other. Got it?"

She nodded again.

"Alright. Let's go," he said, and they exited the vehicle.

They shopped quickly and paid cash.

When they returned to the vehicle, Declan loaded their purchases into the back of the SUV. Mary got back into the passenger seat. Declan got back behind the wheel.

Declan squeezed her hand, started the ignition, and drove out of the parking lot. This time, he took State Route 1 south instead of I-95, preferring to use city streets over the Interstate.

Twenty minutes later, he pulled into the driveway of the safe house. He pulled into the attached garage and closed the garage door with the clicker located on the visor. He turned off the engine and got out.

"Stick close to me while I clear da house, but stay behind me," he said, pulling out his weapon.

Mary got out and followed him inside the house. He moved fast; she nearly had to run to keep up. Having checked the entire house, Declan returned to the garage to get their purchases and the two bags of weapons and ammo that had been in the very back of the SUV.

"What about the other bag with our clothes?" Mary asked.

"I'll burn it later," he said, unpacking the groceries. She sank, dejected, into a kitchen table chair. She laid her head on the table and allowed herself to cry. She felt his hand on her shoulder. "I promise ye I'll keep ye safe, Mary."

"I know," she sniffed. "It's just a lot."

She looked up at him. He nodded. "Are ye hungry? Ye have na eaten since 7:30 dis mornin'," he asked kindly.

Mary shook her head. "I think I'd just throw it up," she answered, taking a deep breath.

"I understand. But ye need to eat," he explained. "A sandwich?"

"Okay. A sandwich," she answered.

He walked back to the refrigerator, where he'd just put the bulk of the groceries. He took out the ingredients and assembled the sandwiches. He sat a plate down in front of Mary. She picked up half a ham sandwich and nibbled on a corner.

"I need to know if my kids are okay," she said. She felt like all the emotion had drained out of her except for fear.

******

"Okay," Declan replied. He retrieved his laptop and set it on the table. He sat beside her and logged in. He pulled up Facebook. "Yer mother's name?" he asked out of courtesy. He had vetted her thoroughly. He knew it was Meghan Cummings.

"Meghan Cummings, or Cummings and Ryan Grocery," she said, starting to shiver. He typed in the info. Sure enough, her mother had posted that she had her grandbabies for two weeks, complete with pictures. "Thank you," she said, her voice quivering.

He rose from his seat and stood behind her, rubbing her arms to warm her, realizing shock was setting in. When he couldn't warm her, he picked her up and carried her to the bathroom. He set her down on the closed toilet seat and turned on a hot shower, letting it start to steam, and then he picked her back up and deposited her into the tub, letting the hot water warm her. He walked out of the bathroom, returning with dry clothes and towels before climbing into the tub behind her, wrapping his arms and legs around her.

"'Tis alright, Mary. I swear, I won't let dem hurt ye. The babies are safe wid yer family. And yer safe wid me. We'll figure dis out." He leaned forward, his cheek against hers as he spoke. She turned her head to look him in the eyes. He turned to her and smiled. She kissed him. He kissed her back.

He looked her right in the eyes. "Mary, I'd like nuthin' more, but yer scared, and yer vulnerable..." he said.

"I know what I'm doing. Yes, I'm scared. But I'm not a

child. I know what I want," Mary whispered against his mouth.

"Oh…Good," he said, peeling off his wet tee shirt.

******

Declan rolled over, put his arm around Mary's waist, and snuggled into her back. He was rewarded with a gentle moan from her sleeping form. He smiled to himself. He felt a cold breeze blow across his bare shoulder. "Don't git yerself into a tizzy. I can na help it if yer dead, and I'm not. I like her," he said to the breeze.

"Does he answer you?" she asked.

"He blows on my shoulder," he answered.

"I know. I saw him do it. Is that crazy?" she continued sleepily.

"No. I was just talkin' to a breeze," he said, kissing her shoulder.

"He likes you, but I think he's a little jealous," she giggled.

"I do na blame 'im. Ye're da mother of his children. And ye are…" He took a deep breath. "…intoxicatin'." He meant it. He'd only known her for 40 hours, but he couldn't get enough of her. The smell of her shampoo, the touch of her skin on his, her soft breath, her brown eyes he could drown in. He reached up and played with a lock of her now blonde hair. He hadn't felt this way about a woman ever. He smiled and shook his head.

"What?" she asked, turning over to face him.

"I'm 36 years old, and I'm fallin' in love fer da first time," he admitted. He wished he understood where this came from. It honestly hit him from out of nowhere.

"How can that be true?" she smirked.

"Don't git me wrong. I've had garlfriends. I've just never fallen in love wid any of dem. But ye, ye'll break my heart, Mary," he announced, knowing it was true. Mary Cummings was going to break his heart. And he was going to let her.

"God, I hope not," she laughed. "I don't want to break

your heart, Declan."

"Hmmm. It's too late. It's bound to 'appen," he smiled, stroking her cheek.

CHAPTER 10

Declan let Mary sleep. He snuck back to the kitchen. He made himself another sandwich and sat down at his laptop. He had scanned the dossier before he'd taken the apartment next to Mary's. He pulled open the file and reread it. Sabah Al-Maghrabi was educated by the Muslim Brotherhood. She attended primary schools funded by the Brotherhood. She attended a high school funded by the Brotherhood. They paid for undergraduate and graduate studies. Further, she had family members among the Brotherhood membership. She was not a member herself, but the connections were too deep to be ignored. He'd seen enough to recognize a radical Islamic sleeper when he saw one. She was one.

He took another bite of the sandwich.

His phone buzzed. He picked it up. The text read, "Sabah Al-Maghrabi and Howard Fox killed with the same gun."

"Where are you?" Declan returned.

"Home."

Then Declan typed, "Gavin, can I ask you a question?"

"Yes," came his cousin's reply.

"How'd you know you were in love with your wife?"

There was a long pause. "I saw her across a room and knew she was mine."

"So, I'm not crazy that I fell in love with her when I heard her voice picking up coffee?"

"No," Gavin responded. "You know when you are in love, Declan. It's not crazy."

"Eamon always warns against involvement."

"Eamon is an old, lonely asshole." Wasn't that the truth?

"So does Gunny. He's not old...I don't think he's lonely... Asshole is debatable."

"Your childhood friend? With that advice, I'm willing to bet he's lonely."

"Secretary was asked to process three files...all related to Egypt...C claimed files not being processed caused Fox's death. Will review with Secretary for brief details in am, but could use a copy of the files," Declan texted.

"Will see what I can do...BTW, ammo was Russian," Gavin wrote.

"Helpful."

He deleted the text chain and took another bite. Sabah Al-Maghrabi was engaged to Vladamir Popov, the son of banking oligarch Fedor Popov, owner of Russian Urban Bank, where the Muslim Brotherhood did their money laundering. Could there be a connection to the bank in those case files?

He finished his sandwich and washed it down with a glass of milk. Not twenty minutes later, Gavin had emailed the files. "Mary Cummings?" he texted.

"Yes. Why? She's been fully vetted."

"Thought she had died two years ago," Gavin replied.

"Oh, no. I checked that. Her cousin, Esmerelda Zamphir, was murdered in a home invasion. Stabbed to death with a long, straight blade. She had Mary's ID on her at the time and was staying in a house Mary owned. Mary was briefly listed as the victim, but it was cleared up within two weeks. DNA confirmed the victim. Think that is connected?"

"Any connection to Walter Bowen, Salvatore Geneli/ Andrei Polaski?" Gavin texted.

Declan opened the files, skimming. "Bowen Tobacco...all three," he answered.

"Theodosia Zamphir Bowen. Mary's cousin. That's who's after her!"

"Cousin? So, she'd know about the kids?" Declan panicked. "Kids?"

"Mary has twins," Declan answered.

"Since when?"

"They'll be three in August," Declan texted.

There was a long pause. "Mike's?"

"She asked me not to tell you."

"I'll keep it to myself, but she has to tell the Davises."

"She's afraid they'll take the kids," Declan explained.

"They're not like that...Mrs. Davis is Mary Constance, Dec. Mike was your cousin."

"Mary's the one I love," Declan continued.

"My wife is my best friend's ex-wife. You love who you love. But that's why she has to tell them. I'll meet you at their house. I'll stand with you both."

"Thanks."

Declan deleted the text chain. He stood, and he packed up all their things before waking Mary.

His phone beeped again. This time text was from Gunny, his childhood friend. "Do you trust Maxine James?"

"No. I only trust a select few. Why?" he texted back.

"Maxine James is an alias. That's Maxine Janovich."

"FML," he replied.

"I have eyes on the family until you get here."

He quickly loaded everything into the Escalade. He returned to the bedroom, where he stopped to stare at Mary for a moment. She was beautiful. "How is it dat I love her," he whispered softly. As no one answered, he sat beside her on the bed and gently shook her awake.

"Mary, wake up. We need te go," he said, handing her her clothes,

"Hmmm, what time is it?" she asked sleepily.

"Two in da mornin'," he replied.

"Why are we leaving?" Mary asked, sitting up and dressing quickly.

"The connection between all da files is na just da Muslim Brotherhood. 'Tis Bowen Tobacco," he hastily explained.

"Theo!" Mary exclaimed, realizing his urgency. "She knows Dani and Randy are mine and where to find them!"

"Aye, we 'ave to go get yer chisellers. Now, come on. I've already loaded da car," he told her.

She bolted up. She ran a brush through her hair, and by 2:15, they were out of the door and on the road.

******

As they raced through the night down a deserted and dark road, traveling east on route 3, Declan explained how Gavin had made the connection to Theodosia. Mary, in turn, explained her relationship to the Tobacco mogul's widow.

"Yeah, Theo is the daughter of my Aunt Berta, my mother's sister. My grandparents, Niall and Nettie Ryan, left my mother and father the grocery store and my Aunt Berta the house Grandma Nettie was born and grew up in. Aunt Berta married Nico Zamphir, and they lived in Florida. My cousins, Esmie, Esmerelda, and Theo, Theodosia, grew up in Florida and really had no connection to Colonial Beach, whereas I grew up in Colonial Beach and spent a great deal of my childhood in that house. Aunt Berta had the same kind of leukemia as Mike. He contacted her and convinced her to leave the house to me. He flew her out to Chicago to write out a will and helped her file it in Florida and in Westmoreland County, Virginia. After Aunt Berta passed, Theo contested the will. Esmie was fine with it. In the end, the will stood, and I own the house. I moved back to Virginia intending to live in the house, but I couldn't get work in Colonial Beach. Meanwhile, Esmie asked to live in the house. She got a job as a waitress at a local diner. She was trying to break free from an abusive boyfriend, some guy named Igor, and I wanted to help. The police said that her boyfriend tracked her down and stabbed her to death, dumping her body at the dump with my ID on her. They had me listed as the victim for a couple of weeks. But my mom got it straightened out. I always suspected Theo told him where Esmie was. Theo's a piece of work. She went to prison for kidnapping and conspiracy…and stabbing someone… the woman was the mother of Dan Bradley's son…Mike's sister's stepson."

"I know," Declan said.

"How would you know?" she asked. He was a spy; she got that. But why would her family's craziness be something he would know about?

He sighed. "Jason is Gavin's stepson. Gavin is married te Dan Bradley's ex-wife. Gavin arrested Theo."

"Oh."

"Dere's more," he said.

"What?" she asked with trepidation.

"Maxine James is Maxine Janovich. She's the stepdaughter of a Russian banker in bed wid da Brotherhood," he said.

"I don't believe that. I've known her for 12 years," she protested.

"I have it from a good source," he insisted.

"Your source is wrong." She looked at him, unable to discern what he was thinking. He let it drop…for now.

"Um…Dere's one more thing…not about the threat…but about…us," he stammered.

"What?" she whispered. Did he regret sleeping with her?

"Mike was…Gavin and I are…um…Gran Da had an affair before he married Nan. The woman got pregnant. She agreed to give Gran Da and Nan da baby. She gave birth te ma Uncail Daithi…um Dave…but she had twins…and hid da garl, Mary Constance. Gran Da found out and has been searchin' fer her ever since. Gavin located her a few months ago. Her name is Connie

Davis. Connie Davis is ma aintin."

"You're Mike's cousin?" she asked. "What the hell? I just slept with my kids' father's…cousin?"

"Aye, but I did na know that at da time. I swear," Declan said. He swallowed hard and waited for her to process the information.

She sighed. "It's okay. It's not like you're my cousin. But Gavin knows about Dani and Randy?"

"Aye, he does, but he plans on lettin' ye tell da Davises about da chisellers. And he says he'll stand wid us when we tell dem," he answered.

"We?"

"Aye, if ye want me, dat is," he said, sounding hopeful. She did want him. She couldn't explain it. It had happened so quickly. She had thought it was a physical attraction, which, obviously, it was. But there was something more, something deeper…something that rivaled her feelings for Mike. How could she have fallen in love with him? She'd never been so relieved at the use of a pronoun before.

"Declan, I want you," she admitted. "I think I love you."

"Really? Oh, thank God. I love ye, too," he laughed, taking her hand.

She couldn't believe the relief and the joy that filled her heart. She hoped Mike would approve. He'd told her that he wanted her to be happy. She whispered, "I'm happy, Mike." She felt an overwhelming sense of peace. She smiled and closed her eyes.

Thanksgiving 2022, Mary had been alone in the Chicago area and unable to make it home for the holiday. Sam Davis invited her to join his family. Mike was very sick by this time. It turned out Jane Goedel had been dosing him with a medication that interacted with his cancer treatment, causing his sepsis. He would die on December 13. But that aside, Mary, who had spent so much time with Mike over that year, went up to his apartment when she arrived at the Davis home that day. He had given her aunt's will to her and asked her to mail something for him after she inherited the house.

He'd asked her to take him down to the gazebo behind the garage. There was a pretty little garden area and a coy pond. In the spring, it had been resplendent with daffodils and roses. Now, there were planters full of mums decorating the area. He told her he loved her. She kissed him. They'd ended up in bed together. She hadn't planned it. But she had fallen for Mike, and she didn't want to lose him. She ended up taking a pregnancy test the morning of his funeral.

"Mary?" Declan said, bringing her back to the present.

"Hmmm. What? Sorry," she responded.

"We're here," he said.

She looked around. Her parents' house was a dark shadow in front of them. "Oh. Okay." He unbuckled his seatbelt and reached for the door handle.

"Declan, a word of warning. My mom and dad can be...a little overprotective," she warned.

He chuckled. "I've stared down terrorists, ma Lovely. I think I can handle yer parents."

"Ha ha," she retorted. "We'll see. But either way, I love you." She smiled.

They got out of the SUV and walked quickly to the front door. The night air was slightly chilly. She wrapped her arms around herself and shivered. He knocked on the door.

A light came on from inside the house. A moment later, the door swung open. John Cummings stood there with a shotgun. Declan cocked his head to the side. "Winchester SX4 Waterfowl Hunter Semi-Auto Shotgun in True Timber Prairie. Nice gun. Would ye like te see mine?"

"Who the hell are you?" her father asked.

"Declan Mahoney. I'm wid her," Declan said, smiling and laying his arm across Mary's shoulder.

"He's my boyfriend, Dad," Mary said.

"Why does he talk like your grandfather, and what the hell are you doing here in the middle of the night?"

"Oh, well, we sent Dani and Randy here te keep dem safe because someone wants to kill yer daughter, only it turns out dat da person tryin' te kill her is Theo Bowen, so da kids aren't safe here, after all. So, we're here to get dem back. Oh, and I sound like dis because I am from Dublin," Declan said, smiling. Mary laughed.

Her father pointed the rifle at Declan.

"Oh, please. Da safety is on," Declan said, pushing the barrel down.

"Come in," John Cummings said, dropping the shotgun to his side and moving aside to let them in.

CHAPTER 11

Declan and John Cummings swiftly moved the twins' booster seats from the Cummings' Ford Explorer to the Escalade. Meghan Cummings carried Dani, and Mary carried Randy. They buckled the sleepy children into their seats. John ran back into the house and came back out with the kids' bags.

Declan suddenly shoved John in the back. "Git in da car! Meghan, Mary, git in! Now!" he yelled. He slammed the door behind John. The women got in as a car came barreling down the street with its lights off. Gunfire erupted, spraying the side of the SUV.

From somewhere behind a grove of trees, someone returned fire.

"Oh, my God!" Meghan shouted.

"Dat one's alright. Dat's ma friend," he explained.

Declan started the engine and threw the SUV into reverse. He backed out of the driveway with the gas pedal floored. He then slammed the vehicle into drive and took off down the road. The vehicle that was shooting at them spun out, trying to give chase.

John climbed into the third-row seat. "How did the bullets not get though the car?"

"It's armored," Declan explained.

He pushed Bluetooth on the dash. "Call Captain America," he told the SUV.

"That's Lieutenant General America," said a man's voice, filling the SUV's cabin.

"Aye, ye win, ye're a higher rank dan I am. Now shut up and let the local police know dat Theo Bowen just shot up da

Cummings' house. I extracted dem, and we're on our way. ETA 13 hours," Declan said, taking a turn at full speed with amazing ease. "Oh, and give Gunny a 5-minute head start to disappear."

"All of them?" the man asked.

"I left da cat," Declan replied.

"Deb's Uncle Tom is coming up behind you. He's got a kit for you. Slow down, but don't stop. Roll down your window for the hand off," said the voice.

Declan did as instructed. A pickup behind them sped up and passed them. Declan rolled down his window. The passenger side window on the truck lowered. A woman John recognized as Ava Bradley sat in the passenger seat. Her fiancé, Tom Mathews, was driving. She held an envelope out the window. Declan merged closer to the truck, reached out the window, took the envelope, and merged back into his lane. Ava and Tom waved and fell back in behind them. Declan handed the envelope to Mary. She opened it, revealing a stack of cash and a couple of IDs. She handed Declan a Virginia driver's license with his picture on it. She took hers out of the envelope and shoved it into her wallet.

"Declan and Mary O'Mally," she said. She shoved the envelope into her purse.

Meghan, hyperventilating, climbed to the third-row seats, where she collapsed into her husband's arms.

"Hand off complete," Declan said to the voice.

"Okay, Major Mahoney. See you in 13 hours."

"Aye, General Mahoney. See ye den," Declan signed off. He looked in the rearview mirror at the kids, already sleeping, and Mary's parents. "Sorry, I hadn't intended to bring ye wid us, but Mrs. Bowen left me no other choice. But I promise, I'll git ye home safe. Right now, I want te know what connection Theo Bowen has te the Muslim Brotherhood."

"The what?" John asked. "Who are you?"

Declan stared at the mirror. He didn't answer for a long

time. John stared back at the steely blue eyes in the mirror.

"Major Declan Mahoney, J2 officer," he said finally.

"What is J2?" Meghan asked, grabbing John's arm. John patted her hand.

"Irish Military Intelligence," Declan replied. His steely blues never wavered.

"And the voice?" John asked.

"My cousin, Lieutenant General Gavin Mahoney, US Army, attached to CID," Declan replied.

"No offense, but why would you care about us?" Meghan cried.

"Mike Davis was our cousin," he said. "Ye're family," he replied. "Plus, I love Mary."

Mary smiled. John knew one thing to be true: Mary loved Declan. Mary trusted Declan. And whatever else was true, Declan looked at Mary like she was the world. The man had just saved their lives. John was willing to give him the benefit of the doubt.

"Where are we going?" John asked.

"Illinois. Mary needs te talk te our aunt. It's the right thing te do. It's time. But more, Gavin's dere and he kin help. He has been helpin'," Declan said.

"I agree that it's time," John said, "but are you doing this under your own free will, Mary?"

"Yes, Daddy. I haven't mailed that letter because I need to do this in person. Now is the time," Mary replied, blinking back tears.

John nodded. She was 31 years old. "You're old enough to make your own decisions, Mare. At least this one has half a brain, unlike that moron Max set you up with last year. What was his name? Pop...something. Had a vampire name."

"You dated Vladimir Popov?" Declan asked.

"No, not really. Max set us up. We went out on like two or three dates. Daddy's right. He was a moron," Mary replied.

"How do you know Vlad?"

Declan laughed and shook his head. "His father owns Urban Russian...da bank dat launders money fer da Brotherhood. And he was Sabah Al-Maghrabi's fiancé," he said. "How exactly do ye know Max James?"

"Max? We met in college. We've been best friends for twelve years," Mary answered.

"Call Captain America!" Declan told the car.

"Yeah?" came the voice again.

"Run a background check on Maxine James, University of Virginia graduate, class of 2016."

"You got it."

They rode in silence for about twenty minutes before the car beeped at them. "Answer call," Declan said.

"Good catch. Maxine James is an alias for Maxine Janovich, born in Moscow in 1995, Fedor Popov's stepdaughter...ex-fiance of Kris Bowen. She's bad news."

"Kris Bowen? As in Bowen Tobacco?" Declan asked.

"Yep. He was a psychopath."

"Was?" Declan asked.

"Dead. 2 years ago," said the voice.

"Are ye certain? Ye thought Mary died 2 years ago," Declan pressed.

"In this case, yes. I saw him die. Uncle Sam shot him in the head. He was...romantically involved ...with Theo."

"Got it. Thanks." Declan said. He looked at Mary, who sat there with her mouth wide open.

"That BITCH!" Mary yelled.

"Mommy?" said Dani, crying upon being awakened.

CHAPTER 12

Connie laughed and took a sip of her Merlot. Her grandson, 10-month-old Sammy, sat on the floor, playing at her feet. Miranda, her daughter, sat on the floor, pushing the ball to the baby. Sammy was learning to push it back. Her son-in-law, Dan, beamed, and her husband, Sam, said, "Good job, Sammy!"

The timer to the oven went off. She set down her glass and rose to go check on the rib roast she had in the oven. She made her way from the family room, through the dining room and butler's pantry to her kitchen. Ghostlike, sitting silently at the kitchen table, her nephew, Gavin Mahoney, waited. She yelped upon seeing him. "Jesus! Gavin! What are you doing in here?" she exclaimed.

"An Escalade will be buzzing at your gate in just a minute. Let him in. It's Declan," he said, almost sadly.

"Declan? Declan Mahoney, Aiden's son? Really! I can't wait to meet him!" she said. "Sam, Gavin's here. He says Declan is about to buzz at the gate."

Sam, Dan, and Miranda, with Sammy on her hip, appeared in the door to the kitchen.

"Ever heard of knocking?" Dan scowled. He and Gavin had been best friends but since Christmas, they had fallen out. Dan had a right to be angry, but Connie adored her nephew. Somehow, he could bypass their security, and she didn't care.

"Don't be silly. You never have to knock," she exclaimed, kissing his cheek.

He smiled...again, almost sadly.

"I know something," he said mysteriously. "But it isn't for me to tell you. Just know, I just found out last night."

The gate buzzed. Sam looked dubious, but he opened the gate. A black Escalade pulled up to the garage. A man, similar in height and build to Gavin, got out from behind the steering wheel. A blonde exited the passenger side. They opened the back seat. They each pulled out a small red-headed child. Connie got chills. Her legs gave out, and Gavin jumped up to steady her. Finally, a couple around her age climbed out from the back. The man handed the child in his arms off to the older woman and opened the hatch at the back, pulling out two bags. He unzipped a bag and withdrew a rifle while the others ran toward the kitchen door.

"Shit!" exclaimed Gavin, bolting out the door. Gavin was fast. He was halfway to Declan, and Connie had concluded the man was Declan in the blink of an eye. Declan tossed the rifle to Gavin and pulled a second rifle out of the bag. Declan dropped to the ground and pointed the weapon toward the gate. Gavin hurdled his way to the hood of the Escalade, using the roof to support the weapon, also pointing at the gate.

Dan yelped behind Connie, drawing his own weapon. The couple, the blonde, and the two children ran into the kitchen. Dan exited, using the pillars of the pergola over the patio outside the kitchen as cover. There was the sound of a vehicle speeding away. Declan rose and ran to a pillar. Gavin followed. Then Gavin and Declan ran into the kitchen. Dan followed and shut the door.

"Who the hell was that?" Dan yelled accusingly at Gavin.

"Theo Bowen," Gavin and Declan said in unison, putting down their weapons.

Connie heard them, but it didn't register. She was staring at the blonde, who hand knelt to hug the two children. Connie's heart skipped a beat, looking at them. "Mary? Ms. Cummings?" she said, clasping her chest, before she sank into a chair at the table. Connie turned to Gavin. "What do you know, Gavin?" she asked, her voice breaking as a sob escaped her throat.

"Mary Cummings isn't dead. And she has something to tell you," he said, looking at the floor.

Connie and her family turned to the blonde. Mary stood and swallowed hard. "Um...I...I'd like to introduce you to your grandkids, Dani and Randy," she said, shoving the children forward. "Dani, Randy, this is your daddy's family."

"Is dat Daddy?" said the little girl, blinking at Gavin, appearing completely lovestruck.

"Uh, no, Honey, that's your daddy's cousin. Your daddy died."

"Oh," she said, blinking more. "He's a pwetty mister."

Declan looked at the child and back at Gavin. "Ye suck! She has na said two words te me," he said.

Gavin shrugged and laughed. "Well, you're not as pretty as me."

Randy tugged on Declan's sleeve. "I tink ewes funty, mister."

"Well, thank ye, Little Man. At least I'm funny," Declan replied, smiling.

"I think *you're* pretty," Mary said, grabbing his arm and looking at him like he hung the moon.

"Should we be calling the police?" asked the older woman.

"Oh, yeah, probably," Gavin said.

Dan took out his phone.

******

Poor Mary was shaking. Declan felt protective, but there wasn't much he could do. He sat beside her on the sofa and held her hand. She squeezed his hand so tightly. Her knuckles were white.

"I'm so sorry," she cried. "I don't expect anything. I'm not looking for anything. I just thought...you should know them...if you want to..." She shivered uncontrollably, and he put his arm around her, pulling her closer.

"It's alright, ma Lovely," he whispered, kissing the side of her head.

"No. Not really," she said, wiping away a tear.

He looked across the table at the crying woman and her husband sitting on the opposite sofa. "I'm sorry. I do na know what te say," he said.

Sam Davis nodded. "You're in the middle. Whether or not it's because you choose to be is irrelevant, I guess."

"How would ye choose, Mr. Davis, if ye were me? If she were Mrs. Davis?" Declan asked.

"You've known her for what? 2 or 3 days?" Sam huffed.

Gavin, sitting on a bar stool, chuckled.

"I'd think you, of all people, would understand how we feel," Sam said to him.

"Oh, I do. Believe me. I do…But I also fell in love from across a room with a girl in a costume. And I loved her for years without knowing her name. Two days or twenty years…love is love. You don't have to forgive her. But maybe listen to her," Gavin suggested. "You're an attorney, Sam. She's the mother of those children. She's offering you a chance to get to know them. How much of a chance do you stand without her goodwill?"

Connie grabbed Sam's arm.

"You're right. You're right. My apologies. Please continue." But anger was etched on his face.

"I took the test the day of his funeral. He'd only just told me he loved me…that I was pretty, smart, and quirky in all the ways that made him happy. And he was all that to me, too…And he was gone, and I was alone…only I wasn't. I just wanted to hold onto that. I intended to tell you. My aunt died. And the mess with the will took forever. The twins were born 4 weeks early… and then Dani was sick. I've carried a letter around that I wrote for three years," Mary explained. Declan gave her a squeeze.

"Dani was sick?" Connie interrupted, sounding worried.

"Yes, she developed an infection in her heart. She's fine now, but I have to watch her and try to keep her from getting the flu. And I focused on that for a long time. When I came back here briefly, it was to get her treated at Lurie Children's. And you were in Hawaii. Then Miranda was attacked…and then you were planning a wedding…and I chickened out. I went back to Virginia…and I don't have any excuse…But I promise they know who their father was, and they know who you all are. I've told them about Mike every night before they've gone to bed …and about you…You can ask them," she sniffed. Her voice broke.

Connie reached across the table and touched her hand. "All he ever wanted was a family. You gave him his legacy… And I love you for it, no matter how long it took you to come to us. I forgive you."

Sam started to protest, and then he looked at Mary. He started to cry. "I always liked you, Mary. So, I'm going to be honest. I'm having some problems with this, but everything my wife said is true. I want to forgive you. Is that enough? For now?"

"Yes, thank you," she said, nodding. She fell into Declan's arms and wrapped her arms around his waist. "And thank you," she whispered in his ear.

"I'll do anything fer ye, Mary. No matter what. Ye're ma garl," he assured her.

"Um…Gavin," said the pretty redhead. Miranda, Declan guessed.

"Hmmm? Yeah, Red?" Gavin said, turning to look at her.

"Deb just pulled up to the gate," she replied, sounding worried.

"What? I told her to stay home! Dec…could you?" Gavin exclaimed, jumping up.

Declan pulled his handgun, racked it, and stood. "Let's go," he said, following Gavin, who drew his weapon as well.

They found Dan in the kitchen, his weapon already drawn,

standing at the door.

"What's she doing here, Gavin?" Dan asked, sounding angry. Declan didn't know what was going on between these two men, but the animosity all stemmed from Dan.

"Jesus, Dan, do you fucking think I'd put her in danger's way…or the kids? I don't know what she's doing here."

The three men exited the door and took positions behind pillars. Deb saw them and the guns. Her expression reflected the fear Gavin was showing. Declan took control and ran across to the 1941 Roadmaster she had driven. "Hello, Deb. I'm Declan. Keep ma body between ye and da kids and da gate. Get dem out, quickly. Unhook da baby before you exit da car. When I run, you run…Understand?" She was a knockout. He hadn't expected anything less. Deb had curly blonde hair pulled up off her neck in a sloppy bun, crystal blue eyes, a creamy complexion, and a killer body. There were two boys and a toddler girl in the backseat. The older boy looked just like Gavin, the younger just like Dan. The baby was clearly Gavin's daughter, also a beauty, Declan noted.

Deb nodded furiously. The older of the two boys unhooked the baby's car seat restraints and handed her up to her mother. Both boys climbed over the seat to the front. Declan stepped forward so Deb could open the car door. She got out, followed quickly by both boys. "Okay. We're going to move…now," Declan said, and he escorted them into the house, followed by Gavin and then Dan.

Once safely inside, Gavin pounced, grabbing Deb by both arms. "I told you to stay home!" he yelled.

"You texted me to come!" she yelled back.

"No…I didn't," he replied, releasing her. "Let me see your phone."

"Are you mad?" she asked, nearly crying and handing him the phone.

"Not at you, mi Vida. Theo's on my list, though," he said,

kissing her cheek and pulling her close.

"Theo? What's that bitch got to do with this?"

Declan caught movement out of the corner of his eye and drew his weapon again, aiming at the older man outside the window.

"Easy, Dec!" Gavin called. "That's Colonel Walters…and Deb's Uncle Frank."

Declan holstered his weapon.

"Uncle Frank" opened the door and came in.

"Apparently, it's a family trait," he said. "The inability for my being able to sneak up on you." He smiled. "Nearly got me shot that time. Major, nice to meet you."

"Aye," Declan said, laughing. "We're one weird ass family."

"Amen to that," snorted Dan.

"Theo?" Deb asked.

"She sent the text, Babe," Gavin said.

"Oh, great. So, this past few days of your sneaking around has been about her wanting revenge on me?" Deb asked. She was clearly upset.

"Not jest ye. Mary as well," Declan said. "Pure feek," he mumbled for the second time this week, looking at a woman.

"Mine," Gavin said.

"Just admirin'. Dat's all," Declan chuckled.

Deb shook her head, curls bouncing. "Mary who?"

"Mary Cummings," Dan said with some derision. "Oh, and not only is she alive, but she has twins…Mike's twins. Guess who knew?"

"Last night! I found out last night! I only gave her a chance to come clean on her own," Gavin proclaimed to his wife, who was giving him a stern look. "Don't look at me like that. Declan knew first." He pointed at his cousin. "He's the one…dating… her."

******

Mary stood at the fireplace, looking up at the family portrait over the mantle. She didn't move when Miranda came in. She just spoke. "He's everywhere here, isn't he? His face, his books…that chess table in the living room. He'd play chess, and all the tics would disappear, and…he could just talk to you." Her voice broke, and she sobbed. "I can hear his goofy robotic laugh…Ha…Ha ha ha…ha ha." She broke down into tears.

"Damn," Miranda said, wiping her own tears away. "I was so going to be mad at you."

"That's okay. I deserve that much," Mary said, tears running down her cheeks.

"Do you?" Miranda asked. "It sounds to me like you loved him, and you were grieving. Mom packed him up. Shut off all feelings. Dad…micromanaged everything. He planned 4 vacations…with detailed itineraries. And I…I let them. On top of losing the father of your unborn children, you had to deal with early labor and a sick child. Grief makes us do…strange things. How about we just…start from right now and let the past stay in the past?"

She took a step closer to Mary. Mary turned to look at Mike's sister, seeing him in her. The tears came fast and hard for both of them. They each just collapsed into the other's arms and cried together, holding on to each other for dear life. Each felt Mike's presence in the other's embrace. Whatever animosity they may have felt washed away in their tears.

Once they had cried themselves out, Miranda took Mary by the hand and led her to the sofa. Sitting, she laughed and said, "So, Declan?"

"Declan." Mary smiled as she said his name. "Declan is… wonderful," she sighed. Just his name filled her with joy.

Miranda smiled, too. "That's great, Mary. Really. I mean, I've only just met him, but I know my family…and he's part of my family. I think he's a stand-up guy. Gavin approves. Dan is mad at Gavin right now, but even he has to admit Gavin is a good judge of character."

"Thanks. I know he's a good guy...It's crazy, but I think Mike approves. I get a peaceful feeling when I ask him about Declan," Mary said, looking at Miranda. She saw so much of Mike in Miranda, the auburn hair, the violet eyes, those freckles across her nose. Her features were naturally softer, of course, but just like with her own set of twins, the similarities were striking.

"I don't think that's crazy at all," Miranda assured her. "You remember that Mike was murdered by Jane Goedel? Amber Gutherie manipulated her on Geno Geneli's behalf..."

"Yes, of course," Mary sniffed.

"Amber is Walter Bowen's adopted sister's daughter. Martha Gutherie. Just so you understand how convoluted this whole mess really is," Miranda explained.

The gate buzzed. Sam Davis appeared at the French doors. "That's the Sheriff. Where is everybody?"

"Um, my parents are in the basement with the kids. Gavin, Declan, and Dan are upstairs, setting up reconnaissance. I don't know where that creepy man is. Mrs. Davis and Deb are in the kitchen," Mary answered.

"Oh, God, Connie's not letting her help cook, is she?" Sam asked, sounding alarmed.

"No. I believe Deb's polishing the silverware," Miranda giggled. She patted Mary's hand. "Our DeBella is drop-dead gorgeous, kind, smart, brave, a great friend, and an even greater wife and mother, but she cannot cook to save her life."

"I'm right here," said the creepy man, appearing out of nowhere behind Mary and Miranda, both screaming at his sudden presence.

Footsteps could be heard running down the stairs behind Mr. Davis. "Frank! Stop it!" Gavin yelled.

CHAPTER 13

"What do you do for a living, Mr. Mahoney?" asked the Sheriff.

"I'm an attorney. I specialize in international law. I am currently retained by the Grand Egyptian Museum in Cairo to help with reacquiring Egyptian national treasures from the Smithsonian...and other museums," Declan said with a straight face.

"How about you, Mr. Mahoney?" the Sheriff asked, turning to Gavin.

"I'm CFO at Fuentes International," Gavin said, also with a straight face.

"And you, Mr. Walters?" he asked, looking at the older man.

"I'm a retired small business owner. I owned and operated 3 restaurants in California," Frank replied.

"Dan?" the Sheriff said in frustration. "What's the truth?"

"The truth is that Miranda's cousin, Declan, drove out to meet the family with his girlfriend and her family, and they were followed," Dan said. His face also revealed nothing.

The Sheriff sighed. "That vehicle is armored."

"Is it? How fortunate! Otherwise, we might 'ave been killed," Declan retorted. Mary snorted. He smiled at her and winked.

"You people called me," the Sheriff insisted.

"Aye, and dat is all I can tell ye at dis time," Declan said.

"Alright, then. All I can really do is make a report that you were followed. If you see them again, call us," the Sheriff said.

"Aye, will do," Declan replied, standing and shaking the Sheriff's hand.

Once the Sheriff left, Sam turned angrily to Declan. "You're too slick by far! We have to live here! Just tell him the truth!"

"I did tell him da truth," Declan replied.

"Oh, just not all of it. Isn't that convenient?" Sam sputtered.

Dan huffed. "He told as much of the truth as Gavin did… or I did. You're not yelling at us."

"I know that Gavin isn't after something!" Sam retorted. "You are my son-in-law. I don't know about…this character."

"What could I possibly want from ye?" Declan asked calmly. He wasn't upset. Sam Davis was angry. He understood that. He'd rather that anger be directed at him than at Mary.

"I don't know, but I don't like you," Sam replied. "I think the truth will come out…one way or another." Gavin looked up sharply at Declan. Declan nodded. He heard the threat, too.

"Okay," Declan said. "I'll do ma best te stay out of yer way den, Mr. Davis. But please understand, dere are things I can na disclose. I told da truth, as fully as I could. I am na tryin' to harm yer relationship wid yer Sheriff."

Sam huffed again and stood, went to his bar, and poured himself a drink, which he took down to the basement, closing himself in his home office.

Mary squeezed Declan's hand. Declan smiled at her and hugged her. "No worries, ma Lovely. Better me dan ye."

"That hardly seems fair, Declan. You're the one who encouraged me to come and talk to them," Mary said, laying her head on his shoulder and snuggling in close.

"Life is rarely fair," he said with a contented sigh. He laid his head on hers, closing his eyes. They sat there, her resting against him, him holding her, and they both fell asleep.

******

Connie stood and covered them with a blanket from the back of the sofa. She motioned for the rest to leave the room. They all made their way to the kitchen, where Connie served the dinner she'd been working on when Declan had arrived.

She adored her husband, but he was acting like a giant ass. Declan was her nephew. And while she had not physically met Aiden, Declan's father, as she had Dave, Gavin's father, she had video-conferenced with her brother in Ireland. He, like Dave, bragged about his son and was a loving father.

There was no way Declan was the kind of man Sam seemed to believe him to be. If anything, he was very similar in character to, only less brooding than, Gavin, whom they both adored. From what she had observed over the last hour and a half, the cousins had a good-natured rivalry. They tried to one-up each other, but there was no animosity between them. If anything, they respected one another. They certainly liked each other.

The extreme disdain Sam seemed to be experiencing toward Declan had begun when Declan had lifted little Randy into his arms and given the child a kiss after the boy presented him with a picture he had made for him while they had been driving shortly after their dramatic arrival. It had caused Connie to feel pangs of sadness, knowing that it should have been her son, not her nephew, lifting the child, but where she had looked on wistfully, Sam had become irate. She was fairly certain that Sam was prejudiced against Declan because he was alive. End of story. And that hardly seemed fair to Declan.

She prepared a plate for Sam and carried it down to his office in the basement. She knocked on the door and called, "Sam, Honey. I have dinner for you."

He opened the door, his cheeks wet with tears. "I won't let him replace our son, Connie. I won't."

"I don't think that's what is going on, Sam," she said, handing him the plate.

"I won't allow it," Sam announced, pushing the plate away. He pushed past her and headed back up the stairs. "Mary, I want to talk to you!" he bellowed.

******

Mary startled awake at the sound of her name being called. Declan appeared to be asleep, but he squeezed her hand and smiled at her without opening his eyes. "It's alright, ma Lovely. Do whatever ye have te do. Dis is yer chance to let the chisellers really know dere father. I'll understand."

"What do you think he wants?" she asked, concerned.

A tear ran down his cheek, and he opened his eyes to look at her. "He wants ye to quit me." He paused and sighed. "I told ye, ye'd break ma heart, Mary. And I knew I'd let ye."

"No. I won't."

"Ye will. But I'll love ye always. Remember dat," he said, kissing her quickly before standing and walking away.

He walked into the kitchen, where Gavin and his wife sat close together, whispering and smiling. His cousin, Miranda, a lovely girl, and her husband were eating at the table along with the children. Mary's mother was at the stove, serving out the food. Her dad was admiring the wine collection in the wine cooler. Sam burst into the kitchen from the basement stairs, his wife following. Mary grabbed his arm. "Declan, I won't," she proclaimed.

"He's na goin' te give me a choice, Mare. He's decided, and I'm made. Ma only choice is te walk away. Ye don't understand. If I'm made, it's not jest me. It's Gavin, too, Gunny, Eamon, and half a dozen others…and it puts ye and yer children in danger, not jest today, but every day fer da rest of yer life. He dislikes me dat much. So ye will quit me. Ye have no choice," Declan explained.

Sam stood there, angry, and nodded.

"Sam!" his wife exclaimed.

"Jesus," Dan said. "I'm pissed at Gavin, but I'd never do that."

"But I will," Sam announced coldly.

Mary sank to the floor. "I should have never come back here. How could someone so heartless have raised the beautiful man I knew?"

"It'll be fine. I'm leavin'. He's not so bad as all dat. He jest does na like me," Declan said.

"Daddy...don't," Miranda pleaded.

"It's too late, Miranda. It's done," Declan said. "I'd 'ave liked te git to know ye, but it's not meant to be. Gavin, I'll leave da car where I got it. Thank ye fer all yer help."

Gavin glared at Sam. "Who the hell are you? I don't recognize you."

"He wants to replace my son!" Sam yelled, pointing at Declan.

"Bullshit!" Gavin yelled back. "Or, do you think I wanted to replace Mark? Get your head straight."

Declan walked out the door and over to the Escalade. He climbed in behind the wheel. Sam opened the gate, and Declan drove away.

CHAPTER 14

Mary sat on the Spanish tile floor until she started to feel cold. She could hear the voices around her, but they were muffled and far away. Mostly, she heard her own heart beating. It felt like it might pound through her chest. He was gone. Declan was gone. She'd only known him for such a short time, but she had fallen fast and hard. Somehow, she couldn't fathom a minute without him in her life. It was more than just a physical attraction, though the physical attraction was...massive. He had brought joy back into her life...not the kind of joy that came from being a mother, but a more personal emotion. For the first time in her life, she felt synchronous with the world, like she made sense in it.

She'd come close to feeling that with Mike, but he'd been so sick. The cancer had been a wall between them that was insurmountable.

With Declan, there was no wall. She felt connected to him, completely...and somehow, she had come to need him in order for the world to make any sense. Without Declan, she was lost.

After hyperventilating for several seconds, she let out a mournful wail that frightened her children. Dani and Randy ran to their mother, calling to her. She grabbed them and pulled them close. "We're leaving," she cried.

"You can't," Connie exclaimed, panicking. "It's not safe." She whirled on her husband. "Why? You're wrong, Sam! And you're chasing her away...with our grandkids!"

"At least he won't replace Mike!" Sam sobbed.

"What? All you've done is make certain we won't be a part of their lives! No one was ever going to replace their father. At the most, he would have filled a void their father left. You can sleep in your office tonight. Once Theo is caught, you can move into the garage!" Connie said, storming out of the room.

Mary pulled herself up off the floor, took a chubby hand of each child into her hands, and followed Connie.

As she stormed away, she heard Gavin Mahoney's voice proclaim, "I warned you, Sam. She is their mother. You broke them up. Congratulations. Now you've lost them. You could have fostered the memory of their father. You'll be lucky if you didn't just wipe it out completely now. She's under no obligation to keep his memory alive."

From the family room, there was a crash and the sound of breaking glass. Connie was halfway to the foyer through the living room. Mary and the twins were a few feet behind her. Everyone else was in the kitchen. There was no one in the family room...or no one should have been in there. Gavin was off like a shot, Dan on his heel. They rushed past Mary and then Connie. They drew their weapons. Gavin went toward the family room. Dan turned to the butler's pantry and half bath.

Dan yelled, "Clear!"

Gavin echoed, "Clear!"

"What happened?" Dan called.

"The big family portrait over the mantle fell and broke," Gavin called back.

"What? How?" Connie cried as she rushed into the family room.

Mary followed. Sure enough, the family portrait lay face down on the floor in front of the fireplace. It had apparently hit the oversized square coffee table that was centered between the two sofas facing each other. Glass was all over the table, the shag rug beneath the table, and the hardwood flooring. The frame broke in the top left corner, but then the wood on both vertical slats was broken through about a quarter of the way down the frame. The portrait itself was crumpled and creased where it hit the edge of the table.

"Fell?" commented Dan, examining the carnage. "It looks more like someone smashed it into the table…with all this damage."

"I agree," Gavin nodded, "but nobody was in here."

His words were belied by a crash from upstairs. The two veteran police officers, Gavin, having been a state police officer for a decade after serving in the army and after returning to school for graduate studies, and Dan, a Deputy Sheriff for just as long, headed toward the sound. "Stay down here," Gavin said to the group, who had gathered behind Connie and Mary. "Frank, make sure everybody is safe."

Frank nodded and motioned for everyone to move back into the living room. Meanwhile, the crashes continued.

Moments later, Gavin and Dan returned. They both looked befuddled.

"There's nobody up there," Dan started.

"Apparently, the pictures are flinging themselves off the walls by themselves," Gavin continued.

"All of the pictures?" Miranda asked.

"No," Gavin said. "Just the ones of Sam."

CHAPTER 15

Declan drove out of the neighborhood toward Kirk Road. He felt like he was dying. Having never fallen in love before, he'd never experienced the kind of heartbreak that had just been inflicted upon him. Breakups had always been a relief, something he had celebrated. He pulled into the Walmart parking lot just to try to breathe. He smacked the steering wheel several times before he let out a mournful cry and buried his head between his hands on the wheel. Mary Cummings had changed him.

He looked over at the laptop. This couldn't possibly just be about revenge. Why had Sabah Al-Maghrabi and Howard Fox been murdered? They had nothing to do with Theodosia Bowen's vendettas against Mary and Deb.

It was easy to understand why Theo wanted revenge against them. Deb, to prevent the kidnapping of her son, had thrown scalding hot Chicken Marsala in Theo's face and then had beaten her unconscious with the fresh-off-the-stove skillet, hospitalizing her for two weeks and forever ruining her looks. Mary's offense was less physically egregious, but she had not bent to Theo's will and had fought to uphold the will left by Theo's mother. It wasn't just the house. Theo had been cut out of other financial aspects as well, those going to her sister Esmie, since Esmie was a waitress, while Theo was married to a billionaire. Esmie had been killed two years ago, purportedly by her abusive ex-boyfriend, but he'd never been located or arrested.

Mary could conceivably be targeted by the Brotherhood through her connection to Howard Fox and her knowledge of the contents of those three files, but that didn't explain the text drawing Deb to the Davis home. Deb had no connection to the

Brotherhood and no knowledge of their dealings.

He was getting a headache. He'd gotten involved in this mess because of the negotiations over the Worker's Contract. That was the only reason he'd looked at Sabah, to begin with. He had not even looked at the research Mary had done yet. He pulled up the file she'd sent him and started to look through it. The Smithsonian possessed the scroll, but they didn't own it. It was on loan from a private collection.

"Fuck!" he yelled, reading the words. The Worker's Contract had been purchased at an Egyptian antique auction in the 1980s by Boban Zamphir Walters. He'd outbid Walter Bowen to obtain it. It had been placed on loan to the Smithsonian in 1998 under the joint ownership of Bob Walters and his niece, DeBella Marie Kaminski. "It *is* the Brotherhood!"

He started the SUV and pulled back out on Kirk, heading back toward the Davis home, calling Gavin as he drove.

******

Gavin answered the phone with, "Yeah?" He was silent while the caller spoke, but the color drained from his face. "Got it," he said and disconnected. Deb knew the emotionless mask he wore hid everything. She had an innate ability to see past the mask. And right then, she saw fear. But he calmly looked up from his phone to hold the gaze of Mary Cummings in his own.

"Mary, what is Deb's name?"

Mary looked confused by the question. It did seem oddly out of place in the current situation. "Um...Deborah?" she guessed.

Gavin closed his eyes and shook his head. He reached across the space between them and took her hand. "No. Her name is DeBella Marie. Her maiden name is..."

"Kaminski!" Mary shouted, interrupting. "Declan was right about the threat being the Muslim Brotherhood."

Deb was taken aback. "Huh?" she exclaimed. "How does

my name tell you that?"

"Because you own the Worker's Contract!" Mary sputtered.

"I own the what?" Deb asked. She had no idea what Mary and Gavin were talking about.

"The Worker's Contract. It's an ancient scroll that was uncovered in the grave of a foreman in the worker's cemetery at Giza. It's one of the artifacts Declan is here to negotiate returning to Egypt," Mary explained.

"And I own it?" Deb asked. "I've never even heard of it."

"Yes. You and Bob Walters," Mary assured.

"Uncle Bob died a year and a half ago," Deb said.

"Okay…so whoever he left his property to…" Mary said. Everyone turned and looked at Gavin.

"I really regret saying yes," he said, shaking his head. Frank patted him on the back.

"I guess he knew you were the best one to handle the fallout from his collections," Frank chuckled.

"But why would the Muslim Brotherhood want to kill me over it? Why wouldn't they just ask to buy it?" Deb asked.

"Honey, the Brotherhood is a radical Islamic organization. They don't want the artifacts to…survive. They consider such things heretical, and you are an infidel," Gavin explained. "Likely, they'd use force to get us to give it to them, kill us, and destroy it."

"I don't understand. Why would they try to get a foothold in the Grand Egyptian Museum if not to display ancient Egyptian artifacts?"

"The Brotherhood recruits through education. They'd want to influence what the museum exhibits to tell the story they want told," Frank interjected.

Gavin's head shot up. His nostrils flared. Deb recognized the transformation. He was a soldier suddenly. He rose without saying a word and bolted up the stairs. He was heading for the stash of weapons. Frank herded everybody to the family room. It was more secure than the living room, which had a set of French doors out to the patio, where the family room was only accessible from interior doors.

Deb hugged Essie close to her chest. Her daughter was just over a year old. Her sons, Hal, the eldest and Gavin's son, whom she had adopted in January, and Jason, her firstborn from her first marriage to Dan Bradley, held onto her for dear life. "Te amo, mi familia," she whispered.

"Te amo, Mama," the boys whispered back.

Mary sat on a sofa, with her parents on either side of her, each holding a red-headed mini-Mike as she grabbed each parent by an arm.

Dan kissed Jason on top of his head. He turned to Miranda and kissed her on the mouth. Then he kissed Sammy on the head. "I'm going to go help Gavin. Be safe. I love you," he said.

"I love you," Miranda mouthed back.

Connie sat with Miranda on the sofa with Deb and the kids and shot a look that dared Sam to sit with them. He sat on a barstool. Deb was worried about them, but in this moment, she was more focused on her own family. If they survived whatever was about to happen, she'd weigh in on Sam's mistake.

Deb closed her eyes and prayed. She prayed for her husband. She prayed for her ex-husband. She prayed for Declan, who, she felt sure, had been on the other end of that call. She prayed that they'd have the strength and the fortitude of mind to protect this ragtag group.

"So much love in one room," came the sardonic quip from the woman as she slowly clapped from the dining room. She stepped from the shadow into the light. She had skin grafts over her face and neck. She was frightening-looking, where she had once been pretty. "Bet you regret teaching me this trick, huh, Cousin Francie?" she sneered.

"Not the best decision I ever made," the older man agreed.

"Aunt Meg, Uncle John, and dear Mary, so happy you could make it. I see you brought the little bastards to meet their father's family," Theo continued.

"Shut up, Theo," Mary replied.

"Mary, you don't get to talk now. Now it's my turn," Theo said, stepping in front of the fireplace.

"Oh, and Deb Bradley…but it's Mahoney now, isn't it?" Theo said with a hideous, evil grin. "Another baby, another husband. And yet, you've maintained your figure and good looks. I can't wait to do to you what you did to me."

CHAPTER 16

Declan, dressed all in black, parked two blocks over and made his way on foot to the back of the Davis's property. The yard was completely enclosed by a wrought iron fence and backed up to a wooded area. He blended effortlessly into the shadows of the trees. He worked his way along the back fence line, looking for where the enemy had breached. Back behind the garage, there was a pretty garden with a coy pond and a gazebo amid the flowers. A section of the fence had been cut and removed behind the cover the gazebo provided from the camera mounted on the back of the garage. Two men, also dressed in black and nearly invisible in the shadows, stood guard at the point the enemy had entered the property.

Declan moved silently. He picked up a rock and tossed it deeper into the woods, away from his position. The guards, having heard the rock, jumped to attention at the sound.

"Go see what that was," said one to the other.

"Be right back," said the other as he moved stealthily off in the direction of the sound. Declan smiled wickedly. He threw a second rock, this time in the opposite direction. When the guard turned to look in the direction of the new sound, he pounced. He grabbed the man around the neck from behind in a sleeper hold and squeezed until he lost consciousness. He pulled the unconscious man into the gazebo.

The guard who had gone after the first rock returned. "Larry?" he whispered. "Where are you?" As he turned his back to Declan, hidden in the shadows, Declan grabbed him from behind and repeated the chokehold on him.

Declan deposited the second guard in the gazebo with the

first. He deftly gagged, tied, and left them as he made his way silently toward the house.

******

Gavin caught sight of the movement from his perch in the attic. He aimed his rifle at the movement and looked through the rifle's sight. Seeing Declan take out the guard, he provided cover until Declan had taken out both guards, tied them up, and made his way toward the house.

Dan quietly moved in behind Gavin and knelt beside him. "Declan just took out the two guards where they breached the fence," Gavin whispered, lowering the weapon. "He'll come in through the basement. It's the easiest and most concealed access from his position."

"What do we do?" Dan asked.

"I'll cover him from here. You go down to the kitchen and cover him inside. Then we'll split up and canvas the house, taking out the mercs," Gavin said. He paused and then added, "Dan, be careful…and thanks for trusting us."

Dan smiled. "You know, you're my blood brother, Gavin, even if I'm pissed. I'll get over being pissed."

Gavin smiled back. "Good to know."

******

Declan hoped Gavin was covering him. He took a deep breath and sprinted to the basement door. Having gotten to the house apparently without alerting the sentries, Declan let out a deep breath and stooped down in the stairwell to the basement door. He deftly disabled the alarm system and picked the lock. As the moon slipped behind a cloud, he silently cracked the door open and slipped inside the inky blackness of the basement. He waited for his eyes to adjust to the darkness. He was in the game room. There was a pool table, an air hockey table, and a bowling lane on the far wall. Declan moved quickly into the next room. Sam's office was to his right. An 84" television hung on the wall directly in front of him. The stairs up to the kitchen were to his left. He pulled his weapon from his shoulder holster and held it in both hands, extended in front of him. His posture was knees bent, his weight on the outside of his feet.

He stopped at the top step. He swallowed hard. He heard movement on the other side of the door. There was a thud, followed by the sound of a body being lowered quietly down the wall. "Clear," came the whisper from the other side of the door. Declan recognized Dan's voice and breached the doorway. He nodded to the right and moved toward the living room while Dan went left into the butler's pantry.

Declan felt the man hit him before he ever saw him. He felt himself slammed into the wall, and the gun fell from his hands. The air was knocked out of his lungs, but he gasped and rallied. He punched blindly and connected with a jaw. He threw a second punch, connecting with the man's abdomen, right in the kidney. He then rushed at the man with his head down, slamming his forehead into his attacker's sternum. He churned his legs until he slammed the man into a table. Chess pieces went flying as they both crashed down on the table, the wood splintering as they crashed to the floor.

A second man rushed him, knocking him off the first. He felt the blade stab his side. He kicked and reached for the gun he dropped. Firing once at the man on top of him and a second time at the man standing up from the remains of the chess table. Both men dropped, struck between the eyes.

Declan grabbed his side and pulled himself to his feet. Knowing the darkness no longer offered any cover, he flipped on the lights and quickly shot at the three men rushing at him from the entryway. He ran, holding his side, through the French doors into the entry and toward the family room. He paused outside the French doors to observe what was happening in the room.

He observed as Theo grabbed Dani from her grandmother's

arms, yanking her to stand in front of her, and held a gun to the child's head. "Who is that?" she yelled. "The Deputy or the state trooper?" She cackled like a witch.

Dani started to cry. Mary screamed for her to let her daughter go. Randy jumped out of his grandfather's lap and rushed Theo, biting her hand. She backhanded the child, knocking him out. Mary screamed, "No!" and tried to jump up, but a man clad in black grabbed her from behind, slamming her back onto the sofa. Declan's heart rate jumped, but he fought the urge to jump in too quickly. He grimaced and held his side, noting the blood flow.

Four other men, one shoving Dan forward, all holding guns, appeared.

"So, it's not the Deputy! We've got him!" Theo yelled toward the entry. Gavin emerged behind the man, shoving Dan and putting his weapon to his temple.

"It's not the state trooper, either," he said coldly. "Put down your gun," he told the man. The man let go of Dan and lowered his weapon. Dan stepped away.

"The lawyer? Interesting," Theo cackled again. She raised her weapon again, pointing it this time at Miranda, holding Sammy. This time, it was Dan and Sam who screamed, "No!"

Declan staggered into the family room and fired. Theo fell. He turned and fired once more, and the man behind Mary fell as he raised his weapon. Gavin pivoted and fired at the fourth man, who also fell dead. The man who had lowered his weapon a moment earlier threw down his gun and raised his hands. Declan fell to one knee, and then the darkness closed around him as his face hit the floor. He heard Mary call his name.

CHAPTER 17

The light was blinding as he regained consciousness, and he groaned in protest as much as in response to the pain that wracked his body.

"Declan!" Mary exclaimed, clasping his hand to her chest.

"Mary," he said weakly. Then he remembered Theo pistol-whipping Randy. His heart jumped into his throat, and he bolted up. "Randy!" he gasped, the pain burning and stopping him. He grabbed his side as he winced.

"He's fine. The doctors checked him out. He has a black eye, but it could have been so much worse. Mom and Dad took him and Dani home in your cousin's and her husband's private jet. They thought it was a great adventure."

He lay back against his pillow. His full memory came back. "Mary! I can't be with you...Mr. Davis..."

"It's fine, Declan," came Sam Davis's voice from the blinding white void beyond the few feet he could see. Slowly, a form solidified, and the room materialized around him, the beeping of the hospital monitor next to him filling the room. "I never would have done it. But I knew you'd have to take it seriously. I owe you an apology."

Declan grimaced again. "Are ye sure?"

"I'm so sorry. You saved Miranda and Sammy. You didn't even hesitate. I was just...I never said goodbye. How could I accept you as their father in his place if I never let him go? I was wrong. And I have to pay the price for my actions. I have to regain my family's trust. That has to start here, with you. I don't expect you to forgive me, but I want you to know I know I was wrong," Sam said, bowing his head.

His pain lessened as a breeze blew on his shoulder. It wasn't cold, but neither was it warm. It was, however, comforting.

"Dere's nuthin' te forgive, Uncail. He says I kin trust ye, so I will," Declan said.

Sam's eyes filled with tears. "You felt him, too?"

Declan nodded. "He's been wid me since I met Mary. That quirky laugh, half a beat off…so ye kin na tell if he' laughin' because he finds the joke funny or jest thinks he should be laughin', mechanical almost…but endearin'. I kin na hear it exactly…more like I feel it."

The Sheriff and another man entered the room. "Mr. Mahoney? Can we get your statement?" he asked.

"Aye. Now is as good a time as any, I suppose," Declan replied.

Mary squeezed his hand tight and kissed him.

He chuckled. "Dat makes it worth 't all," he said.

Sam led her out, and Declan turned his attention to the Sheriff and the man who showed his shield.

"I'm Detective Phil Hodges with the Batavia Police," the man introduced himself.

"Declan Mahoney, Esquire," Declan reciprocated.

"Were you in the military, Mr. Mahoney? I thought Ireland was neutral," Hodges asked.

"Neutral or no, Ireland still has a military. And, despite neutrality, Ireland supplied the NATO-led ISAF mission wid a running total of 120 troops as trainers throughout the Afghanistan war. I served in 2011 in dat capacity."

"Well, that explains it," Hodges laughed.

"Explains what?" Declan asked, shifting in the bed to get more comfortable.

"The similarities between you and your cousin's fighting style. Look, it was all caught on security cameras. We just need to confirm what happened with you," the Sheriff said kindly. Gavin had obviously already soothed over local law enforcement.

"Aye. I left because Mr. Davis and I had a disagreement. 'Tis his house, after all. But I had a bad feelin,' so I went back. Somethin' was off, so I parked two blocks south. I walked back. I saw da men outside by da gazebo. I choked dem out and restrained dem. I went in the basement. Dan met me at da top of da stairs in da kitchen. Da family was being held in da family room. I went through da living room, Dan through the butler's pantry. I was attacked by two men in da living room. We fought. I shot dem both and made my way te da family room, shooting three more, though I do na think I killed dem. In da family room, I killed three more intruders. Da woman had a gun pointed at Sammy and Miranda while holdin' onto Dani. I think I shot her first, then the other two men wid guns on da family. Den Gavin shot da other one...da last one surrendered, and I passed out. I think I was stabbed in da first fight."

Hodges wrote furiously, filling out the statement. "Look it over and sign if that's accurate," he said, handing the paper over. Declan read it and signed.

"So, I'm free te go back te Virginia when I'm released?" he asked.

"Yep. The men who surrendered confessed, and the cameras match your version of what happened. You can pick up your weapon at the Batavia police station," Hodges assured him. "Feel better, Mr. Mahoney."

"Thank ye, Detective, Sheriff," Declan said, closing his eyes. He opened them before the Sheriff and Detective left, though. "One second," he said. "Might I see da blade I was stabbed wid?"

"I don't have it with me," the Detective replied.

"A photo?" Declan asked.

Hodges sighed. Declan had the opinion Gavin wasn't his favorite person...and that the detective's opinion of Gavin

SHENANIGANS: WHEN DECLAN MET MARY 91

extended to him. Hodges didn't like that Gavin was smarter than he was, but he appeared to have accepted that reality, begrudgingly at least. Declan wasn't so sure he'd accept a second Mahoney's intellectual superiority so well.

Hodges sneered but took out his phone and opened a photo, handing the phone over to Declan.

The dagger, a kindjal, from the Caucasus, similar to the Roman gladius, had a ballpoint, double-edged straight blade with an ornately carved wooden bejeweled handle. The scabbard was pictured with the kindjal, apparently having been found on the body of the man who had stabbed Declan. It was silver with an intricate scrolling gold inlay design that flowed into the carving on the handle when the blade was sheathed.

"Georgian?" Declan asked.

"So says your cousin," Hodges grumbled.

"Did you ID the man who stabbed me?"

"His name was Igor Petrov. He was Georgian," the Sheriff said, snickering. Apparently, the Sheriff took great pleasure in the Detective's comeuppance.

"Hmmm. You may want to advise the Virginia State Police. I believe he was a person of interest in the stabbing death of Esmerelda Zamphir, the sister of the bitch I shot in the living room," Declan smiled. "There appear to be older blood stains in the wood carving. There may be DNA evidence connecting this kindjal to Esmie on the handle."

"Why do you think it's her blood?" asked the Sheriff.

"Because Igor Petrov was her boyfriend, and the blade used was a double-sided straight blade with a ballpoint. I read the police reports when vetting Mary for her position as my executive assistant," Declan said, smiling again.

"God damn it," Hodges swore. "Did you really just solve a cold case? You're not even a police officer!"

Declan smiled. "I am just pointing out a possibility. You

are da detective. But if you should discover that 'tis the murder weapon, it can na hurt your career."

Hodges laughed. "I guess you're right. Thanks for the suggestion." Declan knew he'd won over the Detective. The knowledge was gratifying.

After the police officers left, Connie and Miranda paid Declan a visit. "I talked to your parents," Connie said, fluffing his pillow. "And Seamus…"

"Oh, yay," Declan responded sarcastically.

"Declan, they love you," Connie scolded.

"Aye, and I love dem, too. Dat does na mean I want dem fawnin' over me like I'm a five-year-old," Declan asserted.

"Well, they are not coming because they said that was exactly what you'd say," Connie laughed. "But they said they will be coming to Virginia in July." She stared at him for a few seconds without speaking. She looked like she might cry. "Thank you, Declan. You saved my grandbabies. I…I hope you won't hold what Sam did against us. I want to be in Dani and Randy's lives."

"Dat is not mine te give nor take. But whatever influence I may have would be in yer favor, Aintin Connie. Uncail has apologized. I believe him. I think Mary does, too," he replied, reaching out and taking her hand.

She wiped her tears away with her other hand and, breathing through her nose, shook her head, "I swear I wish I had known you all. I missed out on having such wonderful nieces and nephews."

"Ye have us now," he smiled. "And we'll fight fer ye to da death."

"Literally!" Miranda interrupted, laughing.

Declan burst out laughing, then grabbed his side. "Ow!" he exclaimed. "Well, at least two of us, anyway."

CHAPTER 18

Declan and Mary disembarked from the plane. "Ye're certain ye want a life wid me, ma Lovely?" he asked, taking her hand. "Even wid my resignin' ma commission, I'm no prize."

"Declan, as long as I am with you, I don't care about anything else. I believe you are perfectly capable of handling whatever is thrown at you," Mary responded, taking his arm and kissing his cheek.

"Den I am yers, now and forever," he said with a grin.

"Back at ya," she said.

"I'll git ye a real weddin' set after all dis," he promised.

"Like hell, ya will. I only want this one," she said, holding up her left hand, displaying the one they'd put on in the Walmart parking lot to provide a cover while on the run just a week before.

"As ye wish," he laughed, leading her from Dan and Miranda's plane to the waiting limousine.

Gavin and Deb followed them off the plane, then Dan and Miranda.

"Ahhhh…Vegas," Deb said as they all climbed into the limo. "You want to go to the same chapel we went to?"

"Sure," Declan declared. "If it was good enuff fer da likes of ma cousin, it's good enuff fer me."

Dan popped open the champagne in the limo. Miranda passed out the glasses as Dan poured.

Gavin held up his glass. "A toast: To Declan and Mary, may you have the happiness I've found. You'll be truly blessed."

Dan smiled. "Same." He winked at his red-headed bride. "To wedded bliss!"

They all clinked their glasses and repeated, "To wedded

bliss."

******

Mary was gorgeous, whether blonde or brunette, but she didn't feel like herself with the blonde, so her first order of business was finding a hair salon. The Concierge at the hotel recommended the salon in the hotel and Leona Mitchell in particular. Leona was a beauty in her own right, though thirty years older than the bride and her witnesses. Her hair was a beautiful silver and coifed in a stylish bob. Her figure was…elegant was the best way to describe it. She oozed class. Mary liked her immediately.

"Oh my," she scolded, examining the damage done to Mary's hair by the home color kit. "Who did this?"

"My fiancé," Mary snickered.

"Oh, Sweetheart, never let him near your hair again," Leona chirped.

"Oh, I don't know. What came after was pretty good," Mary giggled.

Leona winked and smiled. "Well, some things are worth the consequence, I guess. What do you want me to do with it?"

"I'd like it back to my natural brown and to repair some of the damage…" she offered.

"I'm going to have to cut some. The ends are beyond repair, but if you let me cut it in a new style, I think you'll like it. Something similar to my own style, not quite as short," the beautician suggested.

"Go for it," Mary said enthusiastically, handing herself over to the woman.

Deb and Miranda were entrusted to two other beauticians while Leona worked on Mary's hair. Two hours later, the three women emerged. Deb and Miranda had beautiful curly updos. Mary was back to a brunette. Her hair fell to her shoulders in a long bob, curled under at the ends. It was silky, glossy, and beautiful, and she felt absolutely the prettiest she'd ever been.

Next, they went into the bridal shoppe next door in the hotel lobby. Mary chose a fifties style dress that fell just shorter than tea length with a fitted bodice and flared skirt with layers of tulle. A simple bouquet of red roses, simple white fabric-covered white pumps, and a short veil that fell to her chin completed her wedding ensemble.

Deb and Miranda wore dresses of a similar style. Deb's was a crystal blue that matched her eyes. Miranda's was a sage green that made her auburn hair pop.

******

Meanwhile, the men dressed in matching suits and waited at a table in the bar. They ordered a bottle of Teeling, and Declan poured out three glasses over ice.

"You're sure about this after only a week?" Gavin asked, taking a sip.

"I was sure after an hour," Declan replied.

"Yeah, truth is, so was I. Deb needed more time," Gavin chuckled.

They drank down the bottle. Then the buzzer the chapel had given them beeped. They stood, straightened their jackets, and walked out to the chapel next door to the hotel.

They stood at the front of the small chapel, as Dan and Gavin had done a year and a half prior. First, Miranda appeared at the vestibule and walked down the aisle. Then Deb. The Wedding March started, and Mary appeared. Declan smiled and swallowed hard. She took his breath away. Ten minutes later, she was his wife.

As they flew back to Virginia, Dan asked, "When do you plan to tell everyone else that you actually got married?"

"Soon. Not jest yet. I have to finish dis first. Theo wasn't in charge. She was just along for da ride."

"I agree," Gavin replied, his eyes closed. His forehead was starting to sweat. He groaned and covered his eyes.

"Go ahead and smoke, Gavin. Don't suffer with the headache."

"Alright, I'll go to the restroom. You don't need to be exposed to the secondhand smoke. You're still subject to random testing."

"No. Stay put. I'll go to the cock pit. Declan, come with me," Dan said.

Gavin was pale now and appeared too weak to argue. He just nodded.

"Why? What's 'appenin'?" Declan asked.

"He has Breacher Syndrome, Dec. He needs to smoke medical marijuana…to get rid of the headache," Dan explained.

"He needs what now?" Declan asked, following Dan to the cockpit.

Inside the cockpit, Dan pulled up the video of Gavin in the skirmish that earned him the Silver Star. As the plane was at cruising elevation, the pilot and co-pilot watched, too. The flight attendant joined them and looked over Declan's shoulder. When the grenade went off and Gavin was blown headfirst into a rock cliff wall, there was a collective shocked, "Ohhhh!" Since Gavin had single-handedly pulled 7 people from wrecked Humvees and then engaged the enemy who were attacking, he had clearly earned the accolade.

The pilot asked, pointing toward the cabin, "This is your friend, Mr. Bradley? The guy who flies with you regularly?"

"Yes, Captain Jones, that's Gavin," Dan assured the pilot.

"I know this skirmish," the pilot continued. "My brother was there. Toby Jones. That guy is one of the Lieutenant Mahoneys?"

"Yeah. Is that so hard to believe?" Dan smirked. "One of?" Declan smiled.

"No. The thing is, Toby describes this every Memorial Day. We all pretty much thought he was exaggerating. But I guess he wasn't. I think I owe Toby an apology," Captain Jones pondered.

"Dat's ma cousin," Declan bragged, feeling real pride.

"You were in Afghanistan, too, weren't you, Declan?" Dan asked.

"Aye, at dat time, as well, but further south," Declan replied.

The pilot took out his phone and made a call. "Hey, Toby. – No, everything's good, Bro. I just wanted to tell you that Lieutenant Mahoney is on my plane right now. Actually, I've flown him many times. I just didn't know it was him. – The one in the first skirmish."

Declan blushed.

"The one in your unit that saved your unit. — yeah. – The second one was an Irish Army Lieutenant who led the strike on the enemy forces approaching from the rear, right? He was also named Mahoney, wasn't he?" The pilot looked up quizzically. "Um…yeah, they're both on my flight."

"All I did was call in a strike. He was on de phone wid me when da Humvee hit da IED," Declan said, shaking his head.

"Toby says you also dropped in on a helicopter, personally leading the NATO ground strike that gave them the time to get out of there," the pilot interrupted.

"Don't tell 'im," Declan pleaded with Dan. "He does na remember anything about dat skirmish. It's better dat he not know."

"Why do you think that? Does Horatio know?" Dan asked.

"Probably na. Toby Jones was da communications officer. He knows because he was on da radio. I kept ma name out of da reports."

"Um…the intercom is on," announced the co-pilot.

"Well, shite," Declan said.

He gingerly opened the cockpit door to four sets of unblinking eyes gazing at him.

"Ummmm…" he said.

Gavin quickly stood at attention and saluted.

"Oh, come on. Ye outrank me. Don't do dat," Declan protested, but Gavin was unwavering. Declan had no choice but to salute back, just to get him to stop.

CHAPTER 19

Having separated at the airport, with Declan and Mary heading back to Arlington and the others to Colonial Beach, the newlyweds happily ignored the driver of their limo. Declan poured out two glasses of champagne, and Mary, taking her glass, snuggled down under his arm. She felt like she was on a rollercoaster; breathless, thrilled, a little nervous, but mostly exhilarated.

"Mary Rose Mahoney," she giggled. "I sound like a cliché."

He burst out laughing. He really did have a great laugh, she thought. "No more so dan Declan Brian Mahoney," he said. That accent, those stunning good looks, the single tattoo hidden beneath his shirt like a secret treasure, encircling his upper arm, a testament to a free spirit hidden under a buttoned-up conservative exterior, the steely blue irises that could stare through you but that were softened looking into her own eyes. No wonder she couldn't resist his charms.

"True," she laughed, kissing him. Pulling away, she blushed. "I must say I am not acting very much like myself. I'm not the kind of woman to sleep with my boss and then marry him after knowing him for a week."

"Do ye regret it, ma Lovely?" he asked, looking at her pretty face intently.

"No," she assured him. "I feel alive."

"Mmmm," he said, smiling. He held up his glass. "To feeling alive," he said.

"To feeling alive," she responded, clinking her glass to his. They drank. They set down their empty glasses and wrapped their arms around each other, falling asleep as their driver smiled at them in the rearview mirror.

When they arrived at her apartment building, she rose and sat up, wiping her eyes. "Oh wow, we fell asleep. Hope I didn't snore," she laughed to the driver.

"No, ma'am. But you two were out like a light. I assume you made a quick trip out to Las Vegas from your conversation... Congratulations."

"Thank you," she smiled, shaking Declan's shoulder. "We're home, Darlin'," she whispered.

"Are we? Hmmm. That was quick," he said, stretching.

They climbed out of the limo, Declan tipped the driver, and the vehicle drove away, leaving them standing with their arms around each other at sunset outside the apartment complex. They watched the sun disappear before turning to climb the stairs to Mary's apartment door.

Once they stood in front of it, Declan took her keys and paused. "Word of warnin', ma Lovely. Dere are cameras and bugs in yer flat. Remember Roland Kane? He said we were drinking a bottle of wine on yer sofa. De only way he could know dat was because he saw it on a camera. I'm tellin' ye because I want ye to remember dat and not say anything that will reveal we are onto dem, but ye need to act natural like dere are no cameras. Kin ye?"

She nodded.

He unlocked her door. Then, he swept her up into his arms, kissing her as he carried her over the threshold.

"Oh! So cheesy!" she laughed as he kicked the door shut.

"Perhaps, but I'd never fergive maself if I did na do it," he laughed, putting her down.

She smiled and grabbed his tie, loosening it. "I love listening to you talk, but right now, you need to shut up," she said.

He nodded and put his hand on the small of her back, pulling her against him. She caressed his cheek with the back of her hand as he covered her mouth with his. They melted together into the kiss. She reached around behind her back, taking his hand into hers. She pulled away from him and led him to her bedroom.

Later, lying together, she traced the tattoo, an intricate design of intersecting lines. "Celtic knot...love knot, to be precise," Declan said.

"Did you get it for someone?" she asked, jealousy rising up from the pit of her stomach.

"I told ye; I've never been in love wid anyone but ye, Mary. I've had garlfriends, but not love. I liked da look of it. Dat's all," he explained.

She smiled. "I like that it's hidden under your shirt like it's my own little secret no one knows is there except me."

"To be fair, dere are a few who know it's dere," he chuckled.

"Oh, hush, I'm not that naïve. I know that. I just mean... from now on..." Mary scoffed.

"Now, dat's true," Declan agreed. "I mean it, Mary. Ye're it fer me. I knew it da second I heard yer lovely voice."

"My voice?" Mary laughed. As far as she knew, there was nothing special about her voice. She couldn't even sing all that well. She just had a normal voice.

Declan smiled. "I could na explain it if I tried. It just is."

She laid her head on his bare chest and sighed contentedly.

They heard the door open as Max James entered the apartment. "What the...?" she started, presumably upon seeing the trail of clothing lying on the floor leading from the door to the bedroom. "Mare!" she called, following the trail and nearing the bedroom.

"Don't come in!" Mary yelled. "I'll be right out."

"Is this...a wedding dress?" Max asked from the other side of the bedroom door.

Mary hastily threw on a pair of jeans and a tee shirt from her dresser and opened her bedroom door a crack. She squeezed through the crack, smiled at her once-best friend, and closed the door behind her back.

"Hey, Max," she said, glancing down and picking up Declan's clothes as she made her way back to the door, where she picked up his shirt. "One sec," she smiled, running back to her bedroom, opening the door, throwing the clothes inside the room, and closing the door again.

"'Hey, Max?' That's all you've got? You've been gone without contact for over a week. And you've clearly got a guy in your bedroom. And all I get is, 'Hey, Max'?"

Mary reminded herself to play it cool. Max didn't know that she knew she was the stepdaughter of Fedor Popov, the banker who worked with the Muslim Brotherhood. She needed her to continue not knowing. She fought the nerves, closed her eyes, took a deep breath in, and smiled as she let it out. "Yeah. Sorry about that. I've been…preoccupied," she said.

The bedroom door opened. Declan emerged, rolling up his shirt sleeve. He'd left the top button undone on his dress shirt. The effect was to turn his very formal Italian suit into a very casual but stylish ensemble. He looked dead sexy. Mary's heart skipped a little beat, and she bit her bottom lip when she saw him. "Hello, Max," he said with a smile as he emerged from the hallway. "Nice to meet ye."

Max looked shocked. "Your boss? Mary, this is so…unlike you!" she exclaimed.

"Yeah, well, just look at him…and did you hear that accent?" Mary teased Declan.

He winked…the big flirt. He scratched the side of his nose with his left hand, the wedding ring clearly displayed. Mary snorted.

Max stifled a gasp.

"I'm going to ma flat te grab a few things, Mary. I'll be right back," he said.

Once he had gone, Max grabbed Mary's arm. "OMG, Mare, he's married! Have you lost your mind?"

Mary burst out laughing and held up her left hand. Max stared for a second before she released Mary's arm and grabbed her left wrist instead. "You *have* lost your mind!" Max exclaimed.

"Maybe. But I'm happier than I've been since before Mike died," Mary assured her. She was finding it hard to believe Max was acting. Max was Max. She felt it in her bones. Max was her best friend. Their friendship was real. No question.

"Seriously? You promised to go on a double date with Chaz and me and Rob!"

CHAPTER 20

At 9:34 pm, Declan received a text that the office had been cleared as a crime scene and that cleaners had finished their job, so the office was reopening the next morning. Mary had, of course, left her phone and laptop in the trashcan at the International Spy Museum, so even if the text was sent to her, she would not have received it if Declan hadn't been sitting beside her on her sofa.

"That's quite the coincidence…we get back, and the office reopens the next day," Mary mused.

Declan snorted derisively. "Aye, dat it is. Ye cetch on quickly, ma Lovely."

Morning found them exiting the elevator hand in hand. "Do we need to go to Immigration?" Mary asked.

"Oh, no. I'm a citizen," Declan replied. "I was born in Chicago."

She looked at him like he was a Martian, and they both burst out laughing.

Their laughter drew the attention of the entire staff, some of whom even stood to look at them over the cubicle walls.

Declan raised his eyebrow and got a devilish glint in his steel-blue eyes. He said loudly, "Thanks fer da green card, Mrs. Mahoney."

She laughed even harder. Then he grabbed her and kissed her before walking into his office and closing the door, leaving her to make the explanations.

"You're a wicked, wicked man, Declan Mahoney," she yelled at his closed cherrywood office door.

She felt her cheeks burning as she turned to face the entire office, including the two surviving partners. "He's joking," she said sheepishly. "He was born in Chicago."

"And the kiss?" asked Gloria Nixon, who had been Charlene's second in command and who Mary presumed now had Charlene's job. She sounded every bit as disapproving of Mary as Charlene had been. "Are you really flaunting that you're having an affair with your boss? Because we are revising the employee handbook to reflect no fraternization."

"Oh, it's not an affair. We really did get married. It's not fraternization," she said, smiling and holding up her left hand. Besides, even if it were an affair, you couldn't stop our fraternizing like that. We'd be grandfathered." Mary practically skipped to her cubicle. God, it felt good to put that woman in her place.

Overcome with curiosity, she checked their marriage license, still in her purse from the trip to social security to change her name. His birthplace was indeed listed as Chicago, Illinois. She smoothed it out on her desk and smiled, picking it up and hugging it to her chest.

"You look like the cat who ate the canary," Gloria huffed.

Gloria was Roland Kane's executive assistant and had been in love with him for two decades, according to the office gossip.

"Jealous, Gloria? Want to know how I did it?" Mary asked triumphantly. "It wasn't that hard. I just wasn't a frigid shrew." She deposited the marriage license back in her purse. "Oh, I lost my phone and laptop in the confusion after Mr. Fox was murdered. I need replacements."

Gloria looked like she might explode. Her ears turned bright red. It was hysterical...or at least Mary thought it was. "You...mmmmmeeeep...." Gloria stammered. "Fine. I'll get you replacements. Be right back."

Mary turned to see Mr. Kane glaring at Gloria.

Declan emerged from the confines of his office. "Mary,

see if ye kin git da Egyptian Curator, Maurice LeMeur, te join us today at 11:00 am te discuss when he'll turn over da Worker's Contract te da Grand Egyptian," he said.

"Okay, I'll reserve Conference Room 1," Mary replied. "As soon as I get my new phone and laptop." She turned, smiling coyly, to look at Gloria.

"The Smithsonian hasn't agreed to hand it over yet," she said, stomping her foot.

"Dey do na 'ave to agree. Dey do na own it. It's on loan. The owners 'ave agreed to donate it te da Grand Egyptian...she needs a laptop...now," he said.

Mary didn't think Gloria's ears could get any redder, but they did. She quickly turned and walked away.

Declan handed Mary his phone and laptop and winked. He really was a wicked, wicked man, she thought, laughing to herself.

She had the appointment set and the conference room reserved within minutes. She even confirmed the meeting with Deb, who texted back that they were looking forward to lunch and sightseeing after.

At 10:56, Gloria showed up with the laptop and phone. She smiled wickedly. "IT just got you set up. Guess you can't make that appointment at 11."

"Oh, no. Declan gave me his. We're all set. Thanks," Mary replied, giving the woman another coy smile just as the elevator binged.

From down that marble-tiled hallway, she heard Gavin's voice announce to the receptionist, "Gavin and Deb Mahoney to see Declan and Mary Mahoney."

The receptionist stammered as she confirmed the appointment and directed them to Conference Room 1. The elevator binged again, and the curator and the Smithsonian's attorney arrived.

Then Declan was in front of her. She gave him back his phone and laptop, gathered up her new ones, and stood. He pocketed his phone and deposited his laptop under his left arm, pulled her close with his right, and kissed her again as an extra "suck it" to the rest of the office. She took his arm, and they walked together to the conference room.

CHAPTER 21

The curator was incredulous. How dare Declan attempt to bypass the proper procedures! "I happen to know that the owner died!" he exclaimed. "The Worker's Contract should belong to the Smithsonian."

"But it does na," Declan pointed out. "Please, sit down. Let me introduce the owners. Dis is my cousin, Gavin Enrique Mahoney, and his wife, DeBella Marie Mahoney."

"Your...cousin?" the attorney huffed. "What are you trying to pull?"

"Nuthin'. I assure ye, we 'ave all the documentation to prove ownership," Declan said, shoving a file across to the attorney.

He opened the file and reviewed its contents, including birth certificates, marriage licenses, and divorce papers, and Bob Walters' will. Declan smiled smugly.

The attorney looked defeated. He took a deep breath and revealed part of their hand. "Mr. and Mrs. Mahoney, I understand that there is a buyer interested in this particular artifact. Without revealing too much, she is the widow of a very influential man who had previously shown interest in buying this piece, and she has expressed an interest in the Smithsonian maintaining possession. It would be far more lucrative to sell to her."

Gavin smiled coldly. "No one has made an offer to purchase it. And even if someone had, we wouldn't sell. We want to return it to Egypt."

"You have no idea of the value..." the attorney started.

Gavin sighed. "My maternal grandfather was Enrique Fuentes of Fuentes International. My paternal grandfather is

Seamus Mahoney of Shenanigan Dairy. My wife's uncle was Bob Walters of Walters Furnishings. I don't need money. Turn over the Worker's Contract." With that, he stood and took Deb's hand. "Lunch?" he asked.

Mary grabbed Declan's arm. "Shenanigan Dairy?" she asked. The Irish company produced Irish butter and controlled 60% of the 80% of butter imported to the US that was controlled by Irish butter producers. Additionally, the company had purchased a failing cheese processing plant in Wisconsin thirty-six years ago and was now a leading producer of American cheese in the United States. Thirty-six years ago...and Declan was born in Chicago... "You're like...rich...really rich," she observed.

"Not as rich as him," Declan said, winking and pointing at Gavin.

"After the 10th or 11th billion, is there really a difference?" she asked.

"No, not really," Declan conceded. "Does it change anything?"

"Of course not. Though I'm sure your family would prefer I had signed a prenup," she suggested.

He shrugged. "I told ye. Ye're it fer me. I do na care what dey might want."

The attorney for the Smithsonian smiled a wicked smile.

Despite their fervent objections, they had no choice but to relinquish the Worker's contract. A date and time for the transfer to the Egyptian Grand was agreed upon.

"Don't worry," whispered the attorney as they boarded the elevator. "There's time to convince them to change their minds."

It was when Declan and Mary returned from lunch that it became clear to Mary what the attorney had planned. As they stepped off the elevator, they were greeted by Gloria, looking very smug, a mirthless grin on her face, her arms crossed in front of her chest. "Ah, there you are, Mrs. Mahoney," she sneered. "There is a lawyer waiting for you at your desk...a divorce attorney." Gloria snorted.

Mary was confused, but Declan immediately recognized the man: Horace Gamble. He worked for the Mahoneys. Someone had told his family that he had married a woman he'd just met. He trusted it wasn't the American faction of the family. "Dat snivelin' ferret!" he hissed.

Horace, as they approached, withdrew from his attaché, a contract. "Mary Rose Cummings?" he asked.

"Mahoney," she corrected. "We stopped at the Social Security office to change my name this morning."

He bowed his head and said, "That's fine. Sign Mahoney in that case, where I've marked."

"She'll do no such thing!" Declan argued.

"Calm down, Mr. Mahoney. It's a simple post-nuptial agreement. Your family simply wishes to protect your interests," Horace said calmly.

"I am a somewhat renowned attorney in ma own right, Mr. Gamble. She does na have to sign anything."

Meanwhile, Mary calmly reviewed the contract, picked up a pen off her desk, and signed it. "Your turn," she said, handing it to Declan.

"You did na 'ave to," he protested.

She smiled and kissed him. "I know. I didn't marry you for the money I didn't know you had, Goofy. It's fine. In fact, it's quite fair. Sign it and let Mr. Gamble get back to his own office," she laughed, patting his shoulder.

Declan wordlessly signed and handed it back to Horace.

Mr. Gamble smiled. "Thank you, Mrs. Mahoney. You have no idea how embarrassed I was to have to deliver this. She's quite the catch, Declan. I see why you were ready to punch me. Congratulations to you both."

Mary noticed that Gloria's ears were bright red again. She smiled, took a step closer to her husband, and grabbed his arm. "That ridiculous attorney thinks he can intimidate us by getting your family to turn against me. I don't want your money, my Love. I want you. It's fine. It costs me nothing to sign it."

Declan pulled his arm free and then wrapped both arms around her waist. He hugged her tightly.

CHAPTER 22

The rest of the week passed quickly. Declan, with Mary's help, began earnest negotiations regarding the remaining artifacts on the client's list. He assumed that there would be further attempts to dissuade him, but with Theo's vengeful rampage put to rest, along with her, the Brotherhood would be more subtle. He just had to make certain the artifacts actually made it to the museum and that no terrorist plot revolved around the museum's opening. He was also concerned with who had killed Howard Fox and Sabah Al-Maghrabi. Those murders didn't sit well with him. He was worried about the safety of his new wife and her children.

Dani and Randy were still with Mary's parents, but he and Mary planned to leave for Colonial Beach first thing in the morning to reunite with the kids. Meghan Cummings had gotten Mary's house ready for Mary. Meghan and John professed their approval of the relationship between Declan and their daughter. He had quite heroically rescued them and the twins from Theo and her minions, after all. He was a-okay in their book. They hadn't been told about the marriage yet, though. Mary wanted to tell them in person.

Gavin and Deb had bought a beach house, apparently next door to the beach house that Dan and Miranda had purchased two years ago. As it was Memorial Day weekend, Uncail Daithi and Aintin Gabbie had arrived with Gavin and Deb's kids. Likewise, Aintin Connie, with her husband...he wasn't quite ready to call him Uncail yet, even though he had accepted his apology...Sam had arrived with Sammy and Jason as well, so it was looking like it was going to be quite the family affair.

He had to admit he was a little nervous. Dani clearly

preferred Gavin to him. Randy seemed to like him well enough, but Declan was inexperienced with children. His sisters had some. He'd seen them a few times, but truthfully, he'd never even been comfortable around them. He was a little afraid of breaking them. He adored the twins. How could he not? But he had no idea how they'd take to him.

"Are ye sure dey'll like me? God, what if dey do na?" he'd asked for the hundredth time since they'd left the office just before bed. Mary had kissed him and reassured him that they would love him and promptly fell asleep.

He, on the other hand, was staring at the ceiling for the fourth hour since lying down. Mary grunted in her sleep and turned over, throwing her arm across his chest. He turned to his side to look at her. Her sleeping face was beautiful. He smiled at the simplicity of happiness.

He closed his eyes.

There was a heavy pounding on the apartment door. He grabbed his gun. Mary sat bolt upright, frightened awake by the sound. "What time is it?" she asked breathlessly.

"4:15 am," he answered, climbing out of the bed and jogging to the door. He peeked out the peephole. Crap! Grand Da.

He opened the door wide as Mary emerged from the hallway, looking as befuddled as he felt.

Grand Da, at 87, was still a formidable man...and intimidating. His 6-foot frame still stood as straight as an oak. The cane was really more a fashion statement than a mobility aid. His snow-white hair was still full and lush. He strode through the door with the confidence and bravado of a much younger man. His son, Declan's father, Aiden, followed him, as did Declan's stepmother, Merida. "I understand dat ye are an adult and no spring chicken at dat, but did ye seriously marry a woman ye'd known a week? What are ye thinkin'?" Grand Da demanded.

"Dat it's ma business," Declan answered, sounding braver than he felt.

"Aye. Well, where is she den? Let's see what kind a woman she is," Grand Da blustered.

Declan held out his hand for Mary. She jogged to his side and took his hand in hers. She sure looked cute in her sleep shorts and camisole.

Then the strangest thing happened. Grand Da looked at her, and his expression went from stern to surprised to friendly in the blink of an eye. He exclaimed, "Mary Rose!" as he looked at her, smiling.

"Have we met, sir?" Mary asked, clearly as perplexed as Declan was.

The strangeness continued as Grand Da started laughing. "Ye married Mary Rose? Why did'nya say?"

"Um...I was not aware dat her name would make a difference in yer opinion," Declan said, looking to his father for clarity. His father just shrugged.

"It's not her name! It's her Gran Da, ye eegit. Mary Rose is Niall Ryan's granddaughter!" Gran Da proclaimed. He quickly took out his phone and made a call. "'Ello Gamble – tear up dat post nuptial agreement! His bride is ma dearest friend's granddaughter! Aye, I said te tear it up. Thanks."

"I don't mind having a post-nuptial," Mary shook her head.

"Ye're family, ma gurl. Not some strange woman after our money," Seamus Mahoney proclaimed.

"Am I the same woman I was a second ago?" Mary whispered to her husband.

"Aye," he replied. "Only da king knew ye, so now ye're alright," he snickered. "Ye know her children are ye're great-grandchildren, don't ya?"

"I thought ye only met a week ago?" Seamus said,

confused.

"Aye, but she and Mary Constance's son, Mike, were together before he died. She has twins...a garl and a boy," he told his grandfather.

CHAPTER 23

Declan's Mercedes was nicer and newer than Mary's old Hyundai. So, they moved the booster seats to his car. He was pale and exhausted-looking. His side seemed to be causing him pain. Mary drove. His family followed in the limo. Mary wanted to be home in time for her mother's country breakfast. As they were up at quarter after four, they were able to get on the road by 5 am.

No sooner had they hit the road than Declan fell asleep. As much as she had longed for his company, she was glad he was sleeping. He'd not slept at all overnight, and with his body still healing, he needed sleep. As she neared Fredericksburg, she looked over and saw the sweat on his forehead and the scarlet stripe forming where he'd been stabbed.

She hastily pulled into the rest stop. She jumped out of the car and retrieved the first aid kit and a clean shirt from his bag in the trunk, and walked around to the passenger side of the car. After opening his door and shaking him awake, she got him turned so his feet were outside the Mercedes, and he was facing her. She helped him peel off his shirt. "You've bled through the bandages," she pointed out. "I think you've popped a few stitches."

As she slowly removed the blood-soaked bandages, his stepmother was suddenly beside her. "What 'as 'appened?" she asked her stepson, sounding more than a little panicked.

Mary calmly cleaned the wound. "Yeah, you've torn three or four stitches, Sweetheart. I'm sorry. This is going to hurt a little."

He smiled at her. She knew he was amused by her concern. He'd not even noticed the torn stitches. But he did wince as she used Super Glue to close the wound. She rebandaged the wound and put all his dirty bandages and gauze she'd used to clean him up in a plastic bag. She handed the clean shirt to Merida. "Will you help him with this while I get rid of the used bandages?" she asked.

Merida nodded and mouthed, "Thank ye."

Mary found a trash can and returned to the car. Merida was now in the back seat, between the two booster seats. She had to be uncomfortable, but Mary understood her desire to be in the car with the man she had raised as her own son. "Do you need anything, Mrs. Mahoney?" Mary asked before climbing in behind the wheel after Merida shook her head.

She started the car, and Declan closed his eyes again.

"Call me, Ma," Merida said after a moment of silence. Declan did not open his eyes, but he grabbed Mary's thigh and gave it a squeeze. She smiled silently. She'd won the woman over, even though she had not spoken a word to Mary before this. Mary felt triumphant.

An hour and a half later, Mary pulled into the drive of her Victorian farmhouse. The limo followed her, pulling up alongside her at the edge of the covered front porch. Declan's phone beeped. He glanced down and smiled, handing the phone to Mary. The text read, "Bug and camera sweep clean. Nice house." She handed it back.

He sighed. "Show me te our bedroom, Love. I need an 'our's sleep. Then I'll meet ye at yer parents' home," he said. 'And I bet Ma, Dad, and Grand Da could use a shower to freshen up before meetin' yer family." He smiled. Damn, that smile.

"Hmmmm. Okay," she replied, leaning across the center console to kiss him, lured in by the siren call of that damned smile.

They exited the vehicle. Grand Da and Declan's dad got out of the limo. Mary led her new family inside her house. They walked through the kitchen and dining room. She showed them to their rooms and where the bathroom and clean towels were located, kissed Declan again, and left them, driving over to her parents' house.

******

Declan climbed on top of the antique brass bed, laid his head on top of the pillow, and closed his eyes. He just needed a little sleep. Just a little. The knowledge that Gavin had Frank sweep the house was comforting. And despite the flowery décor of the bedroom and the brightness of the sunshine streaming in the Laura Ashley dressed window, he quickly fell asleep.

The nap was restorative. After an hour, his internal clock roused him. He rose and found the bathroom, washed his face, and quickly shaved. Then he walked downstairs to find his family waiting in the living room. "Are ye feelin' better now?" his stepmother asked.

"Aye, fit as a fiddle," he replied.

"Aiden, Merida, kin I 'ave a moment wid Declan? We'll meet ye out in da car," his grandfather asked.

Declan's parents agreed and walked outside. Once they had gone, Grand Da nodded for Declan to take a seat. Declan sat in an armchair across the coffee table from his grandfather.

"We kin talk here, Grand Da. Gavin's uncail cleared it," Declan said, breaking the silence and revealing the secrets they each knew they kept from one another.

"Yer Aintin Connie sent me da video from her surveillance cameras," he announced.

"Did she now?" Declan responded noncommittally.

"She did," Grand Da said, looking at Declan.

They sat there silently, staring at each other for several more seconds before Declan gave in. "What do ye want me to say, Grand Da?"

"I know J2 when I see it," Grand Da affirmed.

"Do ye? Because I've been wid J2 fer 12 years now." Declan

sighed again.

"Do ye think I did na know? My boy, I've known. And I am proud of ye. I always 'ave been," the old man said. "Do na let yerself become broken. Gavin struggles so. Ye do na 'ave to."

"Aye, he does. And 'tis all ma fault. I was na fast enuff. Five minutes earlier, and I could 'ave saved him all dat pain!" he cried, tears running down his cheeks.

"Jesus, Dec. I was wounded. It was war. You're not responsible. Besides, I've been screwed up since I was a kid. I appreciate that you care, but neither you nor Horatio are to blame for the crap I've lived through. You both need to get over yourselves. I am broken. But I put the pieces back together and keep on living," said Gavin, who appeared out of nowhere. "You need to do the same."

CHAPTER 24

Mary ran from the Mercedes to meet Dani and Randy, who ran from the tire swing to meet her. She dropped to her knees and gathered the two red-headed little cherubs into her open arms, hugging and kissing them.

"Mama!" Dani exclaimed. "I's missed you!"

"Me, too," Randy exclaimed. "I's missed yous, too!"

"And I missed you both sooooo much. Have you had fun at Grandma's house?" Mary was regaled with tales of all the fun things they'd been doing all week as she stood and, taking each by a chubby hand, walked inside the house with them.

She offered to help her mother prepare breakfast, but her mother refused. So, she sat at the kitchen table while her mother made every breakfast food known to man once she settled the twins down in the living room with Disney, Jr. Mary had been there just over an hour when Max arrived.

"Mary!" she exclaimed excitedly, two men following her into the house. "Look who I ran into. You remember Rob Hanson and Chaz Petersen! I thought the four of us could hang out today." Rob Hanson was Max's on-again, off-again college boyfriend. Chaz was his fraternity brother. In the ten years since they'd graduated, neither man had matured much.

Max was still trying to convince Mary that marrying Declan had been a mistake, but this was an especially daring attack, Mary thought.

"No," she said sternly. "My husband wouldn't like that very much."

Mary's mom dropped her spatula. "Husband?" she asked. If Max was expecting Meghan to take her side of this argument, she was sorely disappointed when Meghan clapped and yelled excitedly, "John! Mary and Declan got married!"

Chaz, a meathead of the highest order, flexed his muscles and asked, "Who's Declan?"

"I yam," Declan said from the doorway behind Max and her last stitch gambit.

"This guy?" Chaz snorted. "I could kick his ass."

"No way in hell," Gavin said from behind Declan.

Chaz doubled down. "Look, a Spick and a Mick," he snorted.

"Nice friends ye got dere, Max," Declan said, pushing his way inside. "Breakfast smells amazin', Meg!"

"Thank you, Declan. Come in. Come in," Meghan said, kissing his cheek.

"Did Mary tell ye, ma Ma, Dad, and Grand Da arrived dis mornin'? Dey're on dere way o'er."

"Oh! Wonderful. I can't wait to meet them!" Meghan said, waving the spatula she picked up off the floor.

"I should think ye know dem already. Isn't Gran Da your godfather an' all?" Declan said, stealing a piece of bacon from the stack she had on a plate.

Mary laughed at her mother's suddenly becoming dumbstruck in that moment before Seamus Mahoney appeared in her doorway.

"'Ello, Meg, ma Garl!" he exclaimed, his arms open.

"Seamus Mahoney, oh my God!" her mother exclaimed, dropping the spatula again.

Max hung her head. "I'm never going to convince you that this marriage is a bad idea, am I?"

"No," Mary laughed. "But I still love you."

"What am I supposed to do with Rob and Chaz?" Max asked.

"They can stay if they want. We're just having a big family

get-together. Mike's parents and Gavin's parents are coming over, too…along with Mike's sister and husband," Mary explained.

"I'm so confused," poor Max professed.

"I'll draw out a chart for you later," Mary chuckled.

******

"Hi, Pwetty Mister," the little girl said to Gavin, climbing onto his lap.

"Princess Dani, hello," he replied, presenting his cheek for the child to kiss. He was sitting in one of those folding aluminum lawn chairs with plastic basketweave ribbons beside a keg of beer, sitting in a kiddy pool full of ice.

Declan was there, too, of course, but the little girl had yet to speak more than two words to him. The boy, Randy, at least liked him…or he thought he liked him. He kept pretending to shoot him with his toy gun, so maybe he didn't.

Gavin had kids of his own, Declan told himself. He was nervous around Dani and Randy, afraid that they weren't going to like him, so he was self-prophesizing. At least, he hoped that was the case.

Eventually, he realized that Gavin was laughing at him.

"I do na know how to act around dem," Declan confessed, blushing.

"Just be yourself. You're a likable guy. You're charming and funny, and you sound like a leprechaun. They'll like you. I promise. The truth is, you really are almost as pretty as me, too," Gavin said, bursting out laughing.

"Deccan is pwetty," Dani agreed, "But not as pwetty as Pwetty Mister. See how pwetty your skin is…like candy. Deccan's skin is like milk."

"The kid prefers spicks to Micks," laughed Chaz from the porch.

Declan lit a cigarette. "I'm goin' te feckin' marmalade dat horse's arse afore da day is out," he said under his breath.

"What is a 'horsie arse?'" Dani asked.

Gavin laughed…hard.

"Sumtin, I aught na 'ave said, ma garl. Do na repeat it," Declan snickered.

"Was it a bad word?" she whispered.

"Aye," he replied. "And more dan one in what I said. I wuz actin' da Mickey."

"I's won't tell on you, Deccan. I promise. That man is a meanie." she said earnestly. "Randy is right; you's pwetty funty."

"John 'as explained te me dat dis is Memorial Day weekend," their Grand Da said, approaching with two guitars. "Play 'Green Fields of France,' ma boys. Ye sing like da angels, ye do."

Declan tossed down his cigarette and crushed it with his foot, taking one of the instruments. Gavin put Dani down. "Go get the other kiddos, Princessa."

As soon as everybody had gathered around, the cousins played and sang in harmony.

The song talked about how horrible war is. Chaz took offense.

"Fuckin' foreigners!" he swore.

"Woah," said Max.

"No. I mean it! My dad served in Iraq. None of you served. So, fuck off."

"Grand Da was one of the 2000 Irishmen who served in the American and British Army during Vietnam. He was in the 11th Infantry Regiment. My other grandfather's brother, Jaime, died on November 8, 1965, when the 3,000 came down. My Dad served in Dessert Storm. I was a first lieutenant in the 82nd Airborne in Afghanistan. Declan served as a first lieutenant as one of 200 Irish troops in Afghanistan at the same time. My cousin, Horatio, was wounded by friendly fire in Afghanistan. Be sure to extend our thanks to your father for his service, but unless you actually served, you can shove your opinion up your…arse," Gavin said coldly.

"I've changed my mind. Chaz, you should leave," Mary said. "Max, don't bring him around anymore. Nobody likes him."

Mary stormed off into the house. Declan handed the guitar to Grand Da and ran after her.

CHAPTER 25

Mary reeled around when Declan came in behind her. "I'm so sorry, Declan. That guy is a total prick. I should never have let him stay. I didn't expect him to be that blatantly…"

"No…no, it's alright. Ye're na responsible fer what he says or does," Declan assured her. "But after what ye said, dere is sumtin' I need te tell ye." Declan sat down at the table. He motioned for Mary to sit across from him. She did. He took her hand into both of his. "Dere is one thing dat I was not truthful about. Ye stood up fer a family wid honor. And I can na let da lie stand."

She shifted in her seat. "Okay…" she started.

"Ye asked me if da tattoo had meanin'," he said.

"Oh, well, of course it does. I know that. One tattoo? It means something. Maybe if it was something less meaningful… but a love knot ring…it has to mean something," she responded with a sympathetic smile. She squeezed his hand.

"Aye," he said, his voice cracking and tears spilling down his cheeks. "Ye're a smart one, I should 'ave known ye'd see through dat."

"So, there was someone you loved…" she prompted.

"I never fell in love before I met ye. Dat's da truth. I swear. But I was married," he said, the tears coming faster,

"You're divorced?" she asked, suddenly concerned.

"No," he gulped. "No…widowed." He swallowed hard. He looked her directly in the eye, holding her gaze. "Gavin grew up living like he was middle class. Da Fuentes downplayed dere wealth. Da Mahoneys, na so very much. I attended da best schools. But I was a wild child. I started seein' a garl, Jess McCoy.

Her family was workin' class. She worked in a shop in South Dublin. She got pregnant. She insisted dat we git married. So, I did it. I married her," he said slowly, crying. "It was na good. We were na a good match. Neither of us were 'appy. She had a rough pregnancy. Preeclampsia. She had a stroke at 6 an' a half months gestation. She died. Dey delivered da baby in an attempt to save it after her mother died…" He broke down in heavy sobs. Mary squeezed his hand tighter. He collected himself after a moment and forced himself to continue. "Jess's family abandoned me and da baby, sayin' it was ma responsibility, not dere's. And dat was okay. It was mine. She was…so tiny…just 1 pound 3 oz. She fit in da palm of ma hand." His voice broke again, but he controlled his emotions and pushed on. "She lived 7 days and 14 hours. She died in my hands." The sobs wracked his body now. He couldn't continue. Mary stood, walked around to him, and pulled his head to her chest, her own tears falling down her cheeks.

"Where was your family?" she asked.

He swallowed and forced the response. "I never told dem. I've never told anyone."

"What was her name?" Mary whispered, kissing the top of his head.

"I named her Kathleen Orla. She's buried in the graveyard at St. Columba's Church beside her mother."

"So, the tattoo is for Kathleen Orla?"

"Aye," his voice quivered. "She'd be 18 in a few days."

"Honey, you were just a baby yourself," she said, hugging him.

"I was old enuff," he answered. "I love children, Mary, but dey terrify me. What if I mess up?"

She laughed. "Oh, Honey. You're going to mess up. That's a given. We all do." She cupped his chin in her hand and tipped his head back to look him in the eyes. "There's no such thing as a perfect parent."

"I already taught yer daughter te call Chaz a horse's arse," he extolled mournfully.

She burst out laughing. "I've taught her far worse words than that! Most notably, when a driver cut me off on the beltway, and I screamed…well, never mind what I screamed."

He stood and kissed her. He pulled away from her embrace. He took a deep breath in and exhaled. "I'll do ma best, ma lovely. I hope I kin give dem what dey deserve." He gave her hand a final squeeze and went into the bathroom.

He splashed his face with cold water, leaned both hands on the sink, and watched the water flow from the faucet and circle down the drain. He felt the breeze on his shoulder. He looked up into the mirror. He half expected to see Mike's face behind his, but only his own reflection stared back at him. "I promise I'll do ma best wid your chislers. I'll love dem and be what ye can na be. Do me da favor of watchin' after ma Kathleen Orla. I do na think her mother wanted her in de end. I'm worried she's alone and scared. I can na bear dat."

He expected that gnawing fear to grow, as it always had in these moments of reflection. But this time, all he felt was… reassured. He sighed in relief. "Thank ye, Mike. Tell her I love her. I'll tell dem you love dem as well. We'll be da fathers together we can na be alone."

CHAPTER 26

There was a small knock at the bathroom door. "Aye, I'm done," Declan called, shutting off the water and drying his face with the hand towel. He opened the door to find Randy standing there, tears running down his face, his pants wet.

"I's couldn't hold it," the little boy cried.

"Oh, dat's alright, Randy. It 'appens to da best of us. Let's get ye cleaned up and changed," Declan nodded for the boy to enter. "Do ye need to go more?" The boy nodded. Declan stepped aside and let him in. He found the kids' bedroom and found Randy's clothes in a drawer. He returned to the bathroom and knocked on the door. "Randy, kin I come in?" he asked.

"Yes," came the boy's soft reply.

Declan entered. "I got ye some clean clothes. Kin ye change yerself, or do ye need help?"

"I's a big boy. I can do it."

"Aye, dat's what I thought, sure enuff," Declan said, winking. "I'll jest wait outside da door den." He set the clothes on the hamper and stepped back outside, and waited.

The small voice called from inside after a minute or so, "De...Daddy?"

"Aye?" Declan called back.

"I's needs help wid da zipper." The door opened. Declan kneeled and helped him. "Dere," he said, straightening the child's shirt. "Right as rain."

Randy reached up with both hands and grabbed Declan's face. "I's think yous are a good daddy. Is that okays?"

"Aye, dat's okay," Declan smiled. "Now, tell me ye washed yer hands."

Randy giggled. "Oh, I's forgot!"

"Ye forgot?" Declan laughed. "Dat's manky."

Randy laughed harder as Declan swept him up and carried him into the bathroom. He washed the boy's hands and his own face.

"What's 'manky' mean?" Randy asked.

Declan thought a moment. "Um…ye Yanks say 'gross,' I think."

"Oh," Randy replied. "I likes that word."

"Well, it's a better word dan I taught yer sister, anyway," Declan said, laughing again.

Once they rejoined everyone outside, Randy, holding Declan's hand, said, "Sing another song, Daddy. You's sing good."

"He's Deccan, not Daddy," Dani huffed, crossing her arms and pouting.

"Yous can calls him Deccan if you wants. He and Mommy gots married. That means he's Daddy. He said I cans call him Daddy, and I will," Randy replied. Then, turning back to Declan, he continued, "Yous said it is okay, right?"

"It's okay. And Dani, it's okay if ye do na want te. Ye kin jest call me Declan. And if ye want to call me Daddy later, ye kin. Whatever ye like," Declan told her.

Randy harrumphed at his sister and turned back to Declan. "A song?"

"Aye, alright. Grand Da, ye got yer fiddle?"

The old man nodded, and Declan's father grinned, getting up and running to the limo to retrieve his father's instrument.

Declan took back the guitar as Seamus readied his violin and bow.

"Er Eireann ni Neosainn ce hi," Declan suggested. Together, they played, and Declan sang the mournful song about a fair maiden who vanishes before the singer can kiss her…first in Gaelic, then in English.

It moved Mary to take the guitar, sit in his lap, and kiss him passionately.

Out of the corner of his eye, as it happened, he saw Dan Bradley look at his wife, Miranda, who appeared mesmerized, then walk over to Gavin, still in the chair beside Declan, and smack him on the back of the head.

"Ow!" came Gavin's voice. "What the hell? I didn't do it this time!"

"Wow," he said breathlessly when she pulled away.

Deb, Gavin's wife, shook off her dumbstruck expression and leaned over to Miranda, saying, "Who knew Gaelic would do the trick as well as Spanish?"

Miranda fanned herself and muttered, "They're my cousins. They're my cousins."

Dan huffed and raised his hand again.

Gavin covered his head, ducked, and exclaimed, "Dude, if you hit me again, I'll hit you back!"

"You taught him that trick!" Dan blustered.

"I most certainly did not!" Gavin retorted. "Grand Da taught us both."

CHAPTER 27

Max cornered Mary back at Mary's Victorian farmhouse. Declan had disappeared into the recesses of the house. His parents and grandfather had gone into town, and they'd meet them before the fireworks. Dear God, but Max was determined. Mary didn't know what it was about Declan that Max disapproved of so harshly, but her best friend was like a dog with a bone. And Declan had not dismissed her as a suspect, given her connection to Theo. He didn't seem to appreciate that Fedor Popov was only Max's stepfather and that she rarely saw her mother and her mother's family. Yes, she had set Mary up once with her stepbrother, Vlad. But that had been at her mother's urging. Of course, Theo had attached herself to the Popovs. Wally, Theo's late, old, rich husband, had connections to them. And Theo loved money.

"Why won't you listen to me? He's after something, Mare! You can't possibly know him well enough to love him after two weeks, and he doesn't love you. I'm really worried about you!" Max pleaded as Mary threw a load of laundry into her washing machine. Randy had had an accident at her parents' house. Now that she had the kids with her, she didn't want to leave the wet clothes overnight.

"You're wrong, Max. I love him completely…like I've never loved anyone in my life, even Mike, whom I loved deeply."

"That's lust, not love!" Max argued. "So, he can sing a song and turn your brain to mush."

"I'm 31 years old. I know the difference. And yes, there is lust. Have you *seen* him? But…I don't know…he just fits with me. And you don't know what that song was. His heart was breaking…for real."

"That's bull. Look, Chaz may be a total prick, but he's the prick you know. You know his family. They live down the road. You know he's not after a green card," Max said.

"Declan was born in Chicago. I've seen his birth certificate. And his grandfather is my mother's godfather," Mary refuted. Kathleen Orla. His mother's name was Kathleen Orla, she suddenly remembered.

"How was he born in Chicago?" Max asked.

"Because his parents were in the US to acquire a factory in Wisconsin when his mother went into labor."

"Acquire a factory?" Max scoffed.

"Yes. An American Cheese factory. They own Shenanigan Dairy. He's got more money than you do," Mary retorted triumphantly.

"What if he's scamming you?" Max asked.

Mary sighed and pulled out her phone. She opened Shenanigan Dairy's webpage. She showed Max. She clicked on the CEO link. Seamus's image appeared. She clicked on the President's link. Aiden's image appeared.

"Further, I worked for Sam Davis. Sam and Connie are Mike's parents. Seamus is Connie's biological father. Aiden is her half-brother. Declan is Mike's cousin."

"And that Mexican guy?" Max asked, sounding decidedly less certain of her conclusions.

"That's Gavin Mahoney. He's half Mexican and half Irish. His father is Connie's twin brother...so yes, he is also Mike's cousin...and Declan's cousin. I also know him. He was a client of Sam's."

"So, you're confident..."

"I am confident. And Chaz isn't just a prick. He' a giant prick. So is his father. You can stay if you want, Max, but you need to lay off Declan," Mary said firmly. "I'm done discussing it with you."

"Mary?" Declan's voice called from the living room.

"Coming," she called back. Max followed her through the kitchen and dining room, across the entrance hall, and into the living room. Declan turned and held up a small device, showing her and Max. Then he dropped it to the floor and stomped on it. Max squealed in anguish and grabbed her ear.

Mary's mouth dropped open. He smiled coyly. "Colonel Walters is waitin' fer ye outside. He'll be takin' ye into custody now. Oh, da rest 'ave already been disabled," he said.

Mary sank to the floor. "Max!" she cried. "I trusted you."

"I know. I'm sorry. They made me. I swear," she pleaded as the man Declan called Colonel Walters came in and cuffed her, leading her away.

Declan walked over to where Mary was crumpled on the floor. He reached down to pull her to her feet. "I'm sorry, ma Lovely," he whispered compassionately.

"Is Max really working with the people who are after us?"

"I do na know. Perhaps she is being coerced., but ye can na trust her. Frank will find out, though. Gavin trusts him," he said, pulling her close. He tipped her head up with the tips of his fingers and kissed her sweetly. "It's okay te cry. Do ye want some privacy?" he asked.

She nodded, fighting the tears and biting her bottom lip. He nodded, too. And let her go. She ran from the room and upstairs.

******

"I's seepy," came a small voice at Declan's knee. Dani stood there, rubbing her eyes.

"Aye, alright, den. I'll take ye te yer room," he agreed, taking her hand. He walked her upstairs. At the twins' bedroom, she skipped through the door and climbed on top of her bed. He took the blanket folded at the foot of her bed and covered her up.

"Do ye need anything else, Pixie garl?" he asked.

"Mommy sings me a song," she said, coughing. He reached out and felt her forehead and then the back of her neck. She was slightly warm but not excessively. She probably just needed a nap.

"A song den…Alright," he said, smiling at her. He sang the lullaby he sang to Kathleen Orla during her short life, *Seoithín agus Seoithín*. Dani was soon asleep. He felt her forehead again. He frowned and checked her pulse, which was steady and strong.

He got up, went to the upstairs bathroom, and looked through the medicine cabinet for Children's Tylenol, and, finding none, he closed the cabinet and went to the master bedroom. Mary was not there, but her bag was. He quickly looked through it and found the fever reducer in a side pocket. He hurried back to Dani. He roused her to give her the medicine and then sang to her again, getting her back to sleep.

He rose from where he sat on her bed and quietly left the room. He went back to the Master bedroom to put the Tylenol back into Mary's bag. Mary was sitting on the bed.

"Is Dani okay?" she asked.

"Aye. She's a little warm and coughin'. I gave her some of dis. I hope ye do na mind ma lookin' through yer bag."

Mary laughed. It was musical. "Of course not. All you'd find shocking is my underwear, and you've seen them. You're my husband. You can look at anything of mine you want. Plus, you were taking care of my child."

He lunged at her, knocking her back on the bed and kissing her playfully. She giggled and wrapped her arms around his neck before kissing him seriously.

CHAPTER 28

Declan swallowed hard and took a deep breath. He turned and looked at Mary, sitting in the passenger seat beside him. She was a vision. She had put on a white sundress. Her skin was tanned to a pretty golden hew. Her brown hair fell to her shoulders, just caressing them. She turned to look back at him. "What?" she asked, blushing under his adoring gaze.

"Ye're beautiful, Mary. I like lookin' at ye," he smiled.

"Oh, go on wid ye," she said, affecting an exaggerated Irish brogue and flicking her wrist at him.

He threw back his head and laughed. There it was again: the simplicity of happiness.

"Let's go find ma family," he said, opening the car door. He opened the back seat door and helped Randy out of his booster seat as Mary got Dani out.

"Aren't we your family, Daddy?" Randy asked, blinking his big violet eyes up at Declan.

"Aye, dat ye are. I should 'ave said ma parents and grandfather," he replied, winking.

******

Gavin parked next to Declan's Mercedes. Gavin had always liked old things. He was driving a meticulously restored '41 Roadmaster convertible, painted a nearly black shade of green, the same vehicle Deb had driven to the Davis home the week before.

"It is a nice restoration," Declan noted, running his hand across the hood.

"Thanks," Deb said, climbing out of the passenger seat. "It was Gavin's Christmas gift to me this year."

Declan bowed his head to Deb and smiled coyly. "He has impeccable taste." Then he winked. Deb smiled and blushed.

"I'm standing right here," Gavin said, laughing. "You just can't help yourself, can you?"

Declan laughed and elbowed his cousin.

They walked from their parking spaces toward the High Tides on the Potomac Restaurant, where the Mahoneys had reservations and plans to watch the fireworks from the outdoor patio dining area.

"Mary, these two are insufferable," Deb quipped. Mary giggled.

"I like yer wife," Declan said and winked.

"Yeah, she has her moments. Just don't eat anything she cooks," Gavin retorted.

"Hey!" Deb protested.

"Stolen valor!" came a voice from the crowd on the patio. Chaz Petersen stood up from the table where he sat with a man Declan presumed to be Captain Emmitt Peterson, USAF, Retired; Tom Mathews and Ava Bradley, the couple who had handed off the survival kit to Declan two weeks ago, Captain Jones, Dan's pilot, and a man Declan did not recognize at least not until he stood at attention and spoke when he remembered the voice.

"Lieutenant Mahoney!" Corporal Tobias Jones exclaimed, saluting.

Gavin saluted and replied, "At ease. Nice to see you, Toby. How have you been?"

"Good sir. Thanks to you," Then, turning to Declan, Toby saluted again, "Lieutenant. What brings an Irish Army officer to Colonial Beach on Memorial Day weekend?"

Chaz sputtered, "What the hell?"

Declan returned the salute. "Corporal. It's been a long time."

"I often wondered if you two were related," Toby replied,

laughing.

"Aye, Gavin's ma cousin," Declan replied, reaching out to shake Toby's hand.

"What the hell are you doin,' Toby? These foreigners are fakers!" Chaz scoffed.

"Mr. Petersen, I assure you they are not. I served under First Lieutenant Gavin Mahoney in Afghanistan. He received the Silver Star. He also saved our platoon. And Lieutenant Declan Mahoney served in the Irish Armed Forces in Afghanistan and came to our rescue after an ambush."

Tom Mathews shook his head and stood. He reached out and took Estrella from Deb, kissing her chubby cheeks. "Hello, Essie!" he cooed. "Come see your Great Uncle Tom. Debbie, she's grown!" Chaz looked like he wanted to object, but his father grabbed his arm and shook his head.

"Babies do that, Uncle Tom," Deb laughed. "How do you know Chaz Dumbassson?"

Declan snorted.

"Look here, Bitch!" Chaz accosted her.

"Sit down, Chaz!" the retired Captain bellowed. "There's no stolen valor here. He's a bona fide war hero. His wife has you pegged."

Chaz sat. Tom laughed. "We're neighbors," he replied to his niece's question. "As for Captain Jones and his brother, they're our guests. Ava and I got to know them flying back and forth in your ex's plane."

Randy tugged on Declan's jacket. "Daddy, I's needs to go," he pleaded.

"Aye, alright, den," he said to the boy, lifting him into his arms. Then, turning back to the table, he said, "If ye'll pardon us, we'll be goin'. Enjoy yer meal." He nodded at them and carried his stepson into the restaurant to find the men's room.

CHAPTER 29

Mary looked around the patio and found her new in-laws near the corner by the beach. She waved and excused herself, taking Dani's hand. She meandered through the crowd of tables, chairs, patrons, and serving staff to the table. "Hi, there you are," she said, approaching the table. Aiden Mahoney stood and pulled out a chair for her.

"Ye look beautiful, Mary," he greeted her.

"Funny, that's just what your son said," she answered, taking a seat.

Aiden laughed good naturedly, and pulled out a chair for Dani, then lifted her into the seat. She sneezed. "God bless ye, lass," he said. "Speakin' of ma son…where is he?"

Mary looked at Dani with concern. "Um…he took Randy to the men's room," she said.

"It's nice te see him loosenin' up a little aroun' children," Merida interjected. "He's always seemed a li'l uncomfortable aroun' wee ones. I can na understand it."

Mary's heart sank. Poor Declan. Would his stepmother understand? She glanced down at the table. Merida's hands rested momentarily on her husband's shoulder as he sat down beside her. A glint of gold caught Mary's eye. She looked more closely. It was a bangle…a love knot gold bangle.

"Ma, that's a gorgeous bracelet," Mary said.

Merida looked at it lovingly, touching it with her other hand. "Thank ye. It's precious te me. I lost a son te SIDS. Aiden got me dis bangle in memoriam." She pulled the bangle off and handed it to Mary. "Ye see his name and birth and death dates are engraved inside," she continued, pointing to the engraving.

Mary took it and looked closely. It read, "William Michael Mahoney 7/8/03 – 7-27-03."

"It's lovely," Mary said, handing it back.

"Aye. I was skittish of havin' more children fer a long time," she whispered, leaning her head to Mary.

Mary smiled sadly. Declan was there suddenly. She felt him before she saw him. He pushed in her chair and kissed her cheek.

******

Declan beamed at his wife. She was so beautiful. The twins, one on each side of her, ate their food, Dani barely touching the food, complaining that her throat hurt. Randy ate like a horse, though. Mary smiled back at him.

Dani let out a wail that was startling and frightening. They both turned to look at the little girl, who started convulsing.

"Dani!" Mary screamed.

There was little hope of an ambulance getting close enough quick enough. Declan pulled her out of the chair and laid her on her side. Noticing a piece of bread in her mouth, he grabbed a napkin and wrapped it around his finger to protect his finger should Dani bite down, and swiped his finger in her mouth, pulling out the food. He put his hand on her forehead and said, "She's hot. Has she seized before?" he asked Mary.

"Not since she was a baby," Mary replied.

He pulled off his jacket, rolled it up, and put it under her head.

The hostess ran over. "I called 911. The ambulance can't get through, but the Fire Department is just a few blocks up Colonial Ave," she said, pointing. "You might get her there faster on foot than they can get through the crowd."

Declan looked where she pointed. Dani stopped convulsing but remained unconscious. He grabbed her up in his arms and ran the half a mile, the pavement pounding under his feet. He moved faster than he'd ever moved in his life.

The Firehouse garage doors were open. He ran directly into the building, yelling, "Help! I need help! My stepdaughter has 'ad a seizure! Tonic Clonic. Probably febrile. She's burnin' up."

An EMT rushed forward, pushing a gurney. Declan laid her down on it. "Any history of seizures?" the woman asked, starting to check Dani's vitals.

"Aye, as an infant. She had a heart infection after birth. None since," he panted, leaning on his knees.

Dani started to rouse. "Daddy!" she cried.

"Here, Dani. I'm here," he said, grabbing her little hand.

"Ora wants you to sing, Daddy. She likes that pweety song you sing to her. I's likes it, too."

"Ora?" he asked, shocked.

"See's ma fwiend. See's right dere," Dani said, pointing to empty space.

"Imaginary friend," the EMT said. "Actually, if she wants you to sing, it might help keep her calm,"

"Aye, alright," he said as he started to sing *Seoithín agus Seoithín*.

They moved to the back of the ambulance. Declan never stopped singing and never let go of her hand.

CHAPTER 30

Mary handed the Mercedes keys to Gavin. Her parents took Randy home with them despite his tears. Gavin climbed in behind the wheel while she got into the passenger seat. "Nice car," Gavin said.

"Yeah, Declan likes nice things...kind of like..." Mary started.

"Me?" Gavin asked.

"I was going to say Mike, but now that you mention it... How much did that watch cost?" she teased.

He shrugged. "Grand Da gave it to me."

"So, a lot," she said, sniffing, her voice breaking.

"It's ok, Mary. Declan's with her. He's a medic," he assured her.

She looked at her husband's cousin. "He's a lawyer," she said.

"Yes. So am I. I studied psychology and sociology. Declan studied medicine," Gavin said.

"Declan's a doctor?" she asked. Every time she turned around, Declan was astounding her.

"He has an MD. He never did a residency," Gavin explained.

"You know where you're going?" she asked. He smiled. "Never mind. I forgot who I was talking to." She sat quietly while he drove.

"I wonder why he chose medicine," she pondered after a few minutes.

"Probably because of Kathleen," Gavin said nonchalantly.

She froze. Did Gavin mean the baby or Declan's mother?

He was quiet for a moment. "I mean the baby, Mary."

"Is there anything you don't know?" she asked.

He was uncomfortably quiet. She could tell he was debating whether he should say it.

"I didn't know you were alive." Damn. He said it.

"I didn't know you were anything more than a state cop," she retorted.

"Liar," he laughed.

"Okay. I didn't know until you took down Colonel Boyd and Ivan Yegerov, dismantling the Chicago faction of Bratva."

They rode in silence for another five minutes.

"Does Declan know?" she asked.

He didn't answer. He just smiled.

"I'm just an analyst. Howard was the agent. I really never saw anybody killed before, not even Esmie. And I never thought Theo would come after me," she said.

"How did she figure out you're ATF?" he asked.

"I honestly don't know, Gavin. I swear. I really am just an analyst," she swore. "I started as Howard's executive assistant. Then he recruited me when he learned Theo was my cousin."

Gavin apparently knew his way around the area quite well, as he never used the GPS, and he went directly to the Emergency Room entrance at Mary Washington Hospital. As they exited the vehicle and walked toward the ER door, a woman police officer exited. She pulled up short when she recognized Gavin. "Detective Mahoney?" she said, blinking.

"Hello, Rosa," he said with a smile. "How are you?"

"Good. Um…" her eyes moved to Mary.

"Oh, this is my cousin-in-law, Mary. My cousin came with their daughter in the ambulance from Colonial Beach. I drove her."

"Oh. How's your wife and kids?" she asked.

He laughed. "They're great, Rosa. We're quite happy."

"Well, shoot," she teased. "You're still fine."

"Uh. Thanks," he laughed.

"Take care, Detective," she said, waving and continuing on her way.

"I worked here," he said by way of explanation, opening the door for Mary.

"You're more low-key, but you're as big a flirt as your cousin," she observed.

She walked up to the intake nurse's station. The woman looked up from her computer screen, and Mary asked about her daughter.

"Oh…the singing dad," the nurse smiled.

"What?" Mary asked.

"Oh, sorry. Your daughter keeps asking your husband to sing to her…and he does in some other language…Irish, probably, from the accent. He's got a great voice and that accent…and he's cute, too. We're all very jealous of you," she cooed. "Follow me. I'll take you back."

She followed the woman through a double set of doors and past another nurse's station. She recognized the nurse seated there as a cheerleader from her graduating class at Washington and Lee High School. There was a new high school now, named Westmoreland High School, that opened 4 years ago, but 13 years ago, the county's largest high school had been Washington and Lee, with a second, smaller school in the Town of Colonial Beach. Mary technically grew up outside the town limits and had, therefore attended the larger school some 20 miles away from home in Montross. The nurse's name was Kailey Muse. They hadn't been friends, but they knew one another. Kailey smiled and waved. Mary did the same.

She followed the first nurse around a corner, and there was Dani, small and pale, in a huge hospital bed, with Declan sitting by her bedside, gently rubbing her head.

He looked up as Mary entered. "Dere ye are, ma Lovely. She's alright. Just post-ictal. She'll sleep fer a while. Her fever is down. Her heartbeat is good and steady. Her throat looks red. Dey did a swab for strep. I think the seizure was probably from da fever," he explained.

Mary approached and reached down to feel Dani's forehead. She started crying. He stood and took her into his arms.

CHAPTER 31

Mary cried on Declan's shoulder. She hugged him even tighter. He instinctually understood it was more than her sleeping daughter's illness that was upsetting her. He rubbed her back in small circles. "What's da matter, Mary? What kin I do?" he whispered.

Her arms tightened around him even more. "I really do love you, Declan. You know, there are things I haven't told you…"

"Oh, dat. Don't ye worry about dat, ma Lovely. I know already. Howard told me from da start. Shame on him fer puttin' ye in da field widout da proper trainin'. Thankfully, ye've got good instincts, which is surely what he saw in ye to begin wid," he whispered in her ear.

"Oh, my God," she exclaimed, pulling out of his embrace. "You've been training me. You've explained everything to me every step of the way…what we were doing, why we were doing it…you even took me into the safe house and showed me how to clear it. I thought that was…odd."

"Aye," he chuckled. "I could na believe he used ye like dat widout teachin' ye anything."

"So, you know I work for ATF?" she asked.

"Aye." She stared at him. "Mary, we all have secrets, but I've never lied te ye…except fer that little omission about ma tattoo. Do ye doubt me?"

"No. Just the opposite," she said, sounding like she had made some kind of discovery. "You trust me? Like you trust Gavin?"

"Aye." He was a little lost. What was she trying to say?

"How?" she asked.

He looked at her, her pretty brown eyes staring back into his. "I honestly can na say. I jest do. I loved ye the moment I heard yer voice. I knew…ye're mine. Ye're meant fer me. And ye've never lied te me, Mare. The ATF thing…dat's nuthin'. It does na matter."

She jumped into his arms again and kissed him, taking his breath away. "Don't ever leave me," she said against his lips.

"I won't. Dat's what dat whole gettin' married thing was about," he said, smiling.

"Oh, excuse me. Sorry," Kailey said from the exam room door.

Mary stepped back from Declan, blushing. "No. My fault. I forgot where I was for a moment. Come in, Kailey."

"I just need to check her vitals," she said, grinning.

"Ye know each other?" Declan asked.

"We went to school together," Kailey answered, taking Dani's temperature. "Your daughter's fever is down. Everything looks good. The doctor should be in in a few," she said. "Kailey Muse." She stuck her hand out to shake Declan's.

"Declan Mahoney," he said, shaking her offered hand.

"Mahoney?" Kailey laughed, almost flirtatiously. "That's funny."

"Why?" he asked.

"Oh. I had a criminology professor, Dr. Gavin Mahoney… the credit went to my psych requirement for my nursing degree. He made all the nurses' hearts flutter, too," she explained.

"Aye. Of course, he did. He's out in da waitin' room if ye want te say hello. He drove Mary here. Feckin' Gavin," he laughed and shook his head.

Mary shook her head, too. "Hey, you. They're drooling over you, too."

"No. Really?" he said, realizing that is sort of what the

nurse had said.

"You're 'pure feek,' Babe."

"Am I now? Where'd ye hear dat expression?"

"You said it under your breath when you saw Deb. And…well, I have eyes. I figured out what it meant," she said indignantly.

"Ye googled it."

"That too."

He pinched her waist. "I said it when I saw ye, too." That made her smile.

"What does it mean?" Kailey asked.

"Super hot," Mary replied.

"Oh, yeah. That's right," Kailey nodded. "Your husband's super hot." She winked at Mary.

The curtain was moved aside as the ER doctor came into the exam room. "So, you think your daughter had a seizure?" he asked.

"No, I know she had a seizure. I watched her," Declan replied. He instantly disliked the doctor. His air was arrogant.

"We can't know that without an EEG."

"She had a high fever. She let out an epileptic moan. She convulsed. And she is currently in a post-ictal state. While an EEG, durin' de episode, would definitively prove a seizure, dere is enough evidence te diagnose a febrile seizure widout it. Especially given her history of seizure activity as an infant," Declan argued.

"Where'd you read that, Mr. Mahoney? The internet?" the doctor scoffed.

"*Atlas of Pediatric Epilepsy* by Pramote Laoprasert," Declan countered. "And dat's Major, na Mister."

"Yes, well, I graduated from MCV. I am a medical doctor."

"Oxford University Medical School. Me, too."

Both Kailey and Mary choked on their laughter.

"Kin ye just tell me de results of her strep culture?" Declan demanded.

The doctor stared at him for a moment, then looked back at the chart on his tablet. "Oh. Um…Positive. Is she allergic to penicillin?"

"No."

"Then I'll prescribe penicillin and release her. You should schedule an EEG with a pediatric neurologist."

"Aye. Good call," Declan declared, rolling his eyes.

Twenty minutes later, Declan carried Dani out to the Mercedes with Mary and Gavin following. Mary climbed into the backseat with Dani, who immediately laid her head in her mommy's lap. Declan got into the driver's seat, and Gavin got into the passenger seat.

Declan looked at his cousin. "Ye're na bad lookin' to be sure, but ye're nowhere near as pretty as ma wife, 'Pretty Mister.'"

"Likewise," Gavin laughed.

They drove home in silence. Declan took Gavin to his beach house first. As Gavin prepared to exit the vehicle, he said, "Ya did good, Dec."

Declan smiled. "Thank ye, Gav. We'll talk tammarra, 'ey?"

"Yep. See ya in the morning. Night."

Gavin opened the car door and got out. The porch light came on, and Deb opened the front door. She waved to them as Gavin approached her. Then Gavin kissed her, and they disappeared into the house.

Declan was about to put the car into reverse when Sam knocked on the passenger side window. Declan lowered it. "How is Dani?" Sam asked, sounding mournful.

"She's alright. She has strep throat. She'll be past bein' contagious by mornin', but if any of da other wee ones start showin' symptoms, dey should get checked. Da seizure was febrile. Her fever has broken. Now she's just sleepy," he told him.

Sam lowered his head. "Oh, thank God," he said. Then he looked up at Declan. "That's twice I've seen you spring into action to save my granddaughter. I was so very wrong about you, Declan. I am so sorry. I hope you can forgive me someday."

"Already done, Uncail," Declan replied.

Sam chuckled. "Think you can convince your aunt to forgive me now?"

"I'm Irish born and bred, Uncail. I know damn well na te tell a redheaded woman what te feel. Ye're on yer own dere," Declan said, winking. "See ye tammarra."

Sam waved and backed away from the car.

CHAPTER 32

The morning sun streamed through the slats of the blinds of the two easterly-facing windows. The room was pleasantly furnished in period antiques and modern conveniences. The fireplace stood on the wall opposite the antique brass bed, where Declan turned in his sleep away from the bright light outside, trying to break through the comfortable darkness of his closed eyes. He wrapped his arm around the warmth of Mary's waist and snuggled his shirtless chest against the silky texture of her camisole.

A knock sounded on the bedroom door, and sleep-laden, he thoughtlessly said, "Come in," knowing only his family was in the house with them.

The door opened, and his stepmother stepped over its threshold, holding a set of towels.

"Mary, Love, is it alright to use dis set o' towels?" she asked before gasping, "Declan, ye 'ave a tattoo?"

Mary grabbed his hand, resting on her abdomen, and squeezed. A barely audible "Hmmmmph" escaped her lungs as she realized his mistake at the same time that he did.

"Oh, Lord," he said.

"Is dat a love knot?" his stepmother asked, taking a step closer.

"Uhhhhh...Aye," he stammered. He sat up slowly and rubbed his hand over his dark curls before speaking again. "I guess I need ta 'ave a conversation wid ye and Dad, Ma. Please do na ask me about it right now. Take yer shower. I'll meet ye downstairs in a bit, and we can talk about it."

"Oh...alright den. Da towels?" she asked, sounding more than confused.

"Yes, they're fine to use," Mary confirmed. As Declan's stepmother turned and left, closing the door behind her, Mary turned and sat on her knees behind Declan, sitting now on the side of the bed, facing the windows. She laid her hands on his shoulders and gently rubbed his neck with her thumbs. She leaned over his shoulder and kissed his ear, and then whispered, "It will be okay. I'll be right beside you."

He swallowed and nodded. "Dat was stupid," he chastised himself.

"Eh. You should have told them long ago. Your subconscious just won today," she teased. "I'll go fix breakfast. Bad news is better over pancakes."

She headed toward the door in just her camisole and sleep shorts. He watched her walk away. She had a great ass, no doubt. "Mary!" he called. "Ye're beautiful, and ye're body is a sight to behold. I'd rather be da only one beholdin' it! Kin you put on a robe?"

She stopped, turned and grabbed a chemise off the armchair, and slipped it on. "Better?" she asked indignantly.

"Not much, no, but I think it's as good as I'll git widout an argument," he noted. She tied it closed with exaggerated movements and stormed out of the room, passing Gavin as he walked toward the door.

"You told her to cover up? Rookie mistake," Gavin laughed, leaning on the door's frame.

"Aye, I'm full of dem dis mornin'," he responded, pulling on a tee shirt and jeans. "Did ye git it?"

Gavin held up a manilla envelope. Currier just delivered it. Horatio brokered the deal for you. It can be up and running by fall next year."

Declan took the envelope and skimmed its contents. "Horatio knows what he's doin'. Thanks." Declan tucked the envelope under his arm.

"No problem, cuz. What's family for?"

Declan grabbed his keys out of the bowl on the dresser next to the door. "I never told ye, but I know ye know. I've never been able to hide aught from ye. Ma saw ma tattoo. If ye don't want to catch the fallout from ma mother, ye should leave now."

"Oh. Thanks for the warning. I'll just see you later," Gavin said, and then he practically ran from the house.

Declan understood. Gavin's teenage girlfriend had died pregnant. Aiden and Merida, especially Merida, would surely associate, unfairly, what he had to tell them with that completely unrelated circumstance.

Barefooted, he headed downstairs and to the kitchen.

He sat down at Mary's kitchen table, setting the manilla envelope on the table, and crossed his hands in front of him on the placemat.

Mary ignored him as she scrambled a dozen eggs in a large bowl while butter melted in a large skillet.

"I'm sorry, Mary," he said as she poured the eggs into the skillet.

"Everything was completely covered," she asserted. She was wrong, of course. While the garments technically covered everything, the ensemble was designed to heighten the imagination's picture of what lay beneath the silky fabric. If anything, it was more tantalizing than had she truly been uncovered. But it wasn't worth the argument. Besides, he liked the pajama set. He wanted to continue to see it. It wasn't worth the risk of her no longer wearing it.

"Ye're right. I was bein' domineerin'," he agreed.

"Okay…I accept your apology." She didn't sound certain that she believed him, but he wasn't arguing, so she seemed to have won. That appeared to be enough for her.

Dani came into the kitchen, dragging her blanket and sucking her thumb. She looked small and pale. "Mommy, my throat hurts," she said, taking her thumb out of her mouth long enough to speak.

Mary was in the middle of cooking eggs and looked to Declan for help.

He stood and walked to the fridge, opening the freezer and taking out a box of sorbet. "Here, ma garl. Ye git a special breakfast dis mornin'. It will feel nice on dat sore throat of yers." He set the sorbet on the table and knelt to feel her forehead. No fever, good, he thought. He also grabbed the penicillin out of the fridge door. He grabbed a bowl and spoon. "Do ye want to sit on me or by yerself?" he asked.

"I want you," she answered, holding out her arms for him to pick her up.

He picked her up and sat with her on his lap. "First, ye need te take yer medicine, so ye git better. Then ye can eat some sorbet. Alright, ma garl?" he said to the child.

"Is it yucky?"

"Aye, but one swallow, and it's done," he assured her.

"Will you sing to me?" she asked.

He smiled and sang as he measured out the liquid medicine in the oral syringe before dispensing it into Dani's mouth. She made a terrible face, and he hugged her. "Good job, A stór."

She leaned back to look him in the eyes, "What's that?"

He smiled and kissed her forehead. "It means 'my treasure,'" he explained.

"Is I's a treasure?"

"Aye," he said, hugging her again. Then he spooned out some sorbet into the bowl and pushed the bowl to her. "Try te eat some."

She ate, wincing with each bite and then showing relief as the frozen treat melted down her throat.

Mary finished the eggs and took Dani from Declan, carrying her to the living room, where she deposited her on the sofa in front of the television before returning to the kitchen.

Aiden, Merida, and Grand Da entered the kitchen together. "Breakfast looks delicious, Mary," Merida said, sitting beside Declan.

After they had eaten and cleared the table. Declan slid the envelope to his grandfather. Seamus looked through the documents and nodded. "Are ye certain, Declan?"

"Aye. I'm done, Grand Da. As soon as Mary and I finish dis job. Horatio Fuentes started brokering da deal in Sterling dis mornin'. The Fuentes Building can be converted to a processing plant. It's just sittin' dere empty. It's close enough te our Wisconsin plant te make use of our current resources, and far enough away te be a viable expansion opportunity. The area has a ready workforce. With some modernization, we kin have the plant up and running by next fall."

"And ye're willin' to become President of US Operations?" Seamus asked.

"I am. Ye want te know what I learned over dis two weeks? Happiness is simplicity. It's time to stop runnin' away from it," Declan assured him.

Aiden clapped loudly. "About time, too! Welcome aboard, Son!"

Mary sat quietly, watching this all unfold. Just like that, her new husband was an international Fortune 500 company executive. She pondered his abilities. He was an attorney, a spy, a soldier, an officer, a doctor, and now an executive. "What's your IQ?" she asked, startling herself as she hadn't intended for the question to be out loud.

"Dependin' upon the test, between 140 and 160," he answered as she covered her embarrassment by unfortunately taking a sip of orange juice, which she promptly choked on.

"That's like Einstein level!" she exclaimed.

"No. Einstein was between 160 and 180," he replied.

"Besides, it's just an arbitrary number. It really does na mean anything."

Declan's stepmother had sat patiently through the business, but she was losing patience. She had married Aiden after his wife had passed away when Declan and his two sisters were kids. She and Aiden had a 15-year-old daughter of their own as well. And there had, of course, been the baby son that they'd lost. "I want to know when you got dat lovely tattoo. Is it fer yer brother? It's like my bangle, eh?"

Mary grabbed Declan's hand.

"Tattoo?" his father asked.

Declan rolled his tee shirt sleeve up to reveal the love knot ring around the top of his bicep. He reached into his pocket and pulled out his keys. He held up his key ring. A pewter rectangle with a gold-plated claddagh riveted to it. He pulled off a cap, revealing it to be a USB thumb drive.

"Yes, I chose it because it is similar te yer bangle, Ma. No, it is na fer William. It's fer Kathleen Orla."

"Yer mother?" Merida asked, furrowing her brow.

He took a deep breath and let it out. "My daughter."

"Your who now?" his father said.

"A long time ago, I was involved wid a garl named Jess McCoy. She got pregnant."

"Ye mean, ye got her pregnant," his stepmother corrected.

"Aye," he agreed, "I got her pregnant. I also married her. She had a stroke at 6 and a half months gestation. She died. The doctors delivered Kathleen, tryin' to save her. But it was just too early. She lived 7 days and 14 hours. Dey are buried next to each other at St. Columba's. Here," he said, holding up the USB, "are all the pictures I have of her. I carry her wid me always."

"Jess McCoy? I don't remember da name. When was dis?" his stepmother bemoaned.

"I was eighteen. Kathleen would be 18 next week."

"Oh! A stór. Why would ye suffer dat alone?" his stepmother cried, then kissing his cheek and leaning her head against his. He started crying and wrapped his arms around his stepmother's waist, burying his head in her shoulder. Mary found herself pondering the fact that even spies need their mommies. But the story also gave her chills.

CHAPTER 33

Declan closed the bedroom door behind him. Mary was making the bed before heading to the shower. She was still wearing that pajama set and the chemise. He walked up behind her as she reached for the duvet. He put one hand on her waist. He moved her hair off her neck with the other. He leaned down and just brushed his lips down her neck from just under her ear all the way to her shoulder. Then he reached around and untied the belt to the chemise.

"Oh," she whispered, leaning back against him.

"I like da pajamas, Mary. I like dem a great deal," he said softly against the nape of her neck.

A small knock sounded on the door, and Randy called from the other side of it. "Mommy, Daddy. I's home."

Then Mary's mother called out from the bottom of the stairs, "Mary, Declan! Dad needs help getting ice and the kegs. Oh, and can we move Dani up to your room and put on the races in the living room?"

"Sure, Mom. Declan just needs to get in the shower. He'll be down in five minutes," Mary called, pulling out of Declan's arms and opening the door to her son. "Hi, baby," she said, swooping him up into her arms and covering his face in kisses.

Declan hung his head and moved toward the master bathroom door beside the fireplace. "Cold shower 'tis den."

Five minutes later, he bounded down the steps to find his father-in-law and Gavin in deep conversation about Fuentes International wrenches and how they're the best in the world.

As John Cummings led the two cousins out to his 1971 Ford F150, Gavin looked over at Declan and asked, "Why is your hair wet?"

"Cold shower," Declan mumbled.

"Ahhh," Gavin replied.

"Randy knocked on da door while…"

"Well, at least he knocked…" Gavin commiserated.

"Wait, dere are times when dey do na knock?" Declan exclaimed, horrified at the thought.

"Jason walked in the first night…and then announced to Dan the next morning that I had been kissing his mommy in her bedroom and that she put on my shirt to go get him water."

"Oh, Jesus," Declan said.

"Mary and Joseph," Gavin finished. "Over Christmas, he announced to the entire house that Deb and I were awake and just wrestling in a blanket fort."

"Perhaps ye should be lockin' yer bedroom door," Declan snorted.

"She won't let me. She doesn't want the kids locking their doors. So, she won't let me lock ours."

Halfway to the truck, Randy came running out the kitchen door. "Daddy! Wait for me! I's wants to goes with you," His little legs were churning. Declan swept him up and spun around with him.

"Sure enuff, wee man." Then he tossed the boy over his shoulder. "Ye got room fer dis sack of potatoes?" he joked.

John laughed. "I think we do."

At Cummings and Ryan Grocery, John pulled up to the loading dock. He beeped his horn, and a young man appeared from inside the bay. "Hey, Mr. Cummings, watcha need?"

"Hey, Todd. We're here for the ice and kegs I set aside. Can you help my son-in-law and his cousin there get it loaded into the truck? Randy and I are headin' inside to pick out some ice cream for him and his sister."

John and Randy, holding hands, disappeared into the

grocery store.

Declan and Gavin climbed out of the truck cab.

Todd reached out a friendly hand. "So, which one of you lucky gents married Mary, ey?" he joked, shaking their hands.

"Dat would be me," Declan said, winking.

"Y'all really cousins?"

"Aye, don't we look alike?" Declan teased.

"Dec," Gavin said, sticking out his chin, "Cállate, culo."

"Oddly, ya kinda do," Todd laughed.

"Our fathers are brothers. My mother is Mexican American...his is Irish aristocracy," Gavin explained as they followed Todd to where John had set aside two kegs, one of Guiness, the other Miller.

"I'll grab a dolly," Todd offered.

"Eh, no need. We got it," Gavin said. They each lifted a keg to their shoulder and carried it back to the truck.

"Dang," Todd observed. He grabbed a dolly anyway and started loading several large bags of ice on it. By the time he got back to the truck, Declan and Gavin had loaded the kegs into the back and were standing outside the bay, smoking together, leaning against the brick exterior wall.

Chaz Petersen appeared from around the side of the building, carrying a machete. He raised it and started swinging indiscriminately. He slashed two employees unloading a delivery truck. Declan tossed his cigarette one way, Gavin throwing his the other. Todd dropped to the concrete floor, as did the other half a dozen employees in the bay area.

Declan and Gavin jumped off the raised dock and rushed the crazed man. Gavin clotheslined Chaz while Declan swept his feet. They both dropped their elbows into his abdomen as he landed hard on his back. Declan grabbed the machete and tossed it as Gavin threw Chaz to his stomach, pinning his hands behind his back and twisting his arms to an uncomfortable and immobilizing position. Declan deftly removed Chaz's belt and used it as a make-do hand restraint. All the while, Chaz was screaming, "Y'all aren't real. You're evil spirits masquerading as heroes. You're smoke and mirrors, and the vapor will dissipate, and y'all will be revealed as lizards preying on the blood of children!"

"Call 911!" the two cousins yelled in unison.

"Dang," Todd repeated.

"Feckin' arse!" Declan exclaimed. "What da hell is wrong wid ye?"

"Meth would be my guess," Gavin replied. "And a deep dive into conspiracy theories while on Meth."

"That was awesome," Todd exclaimed. The two men turned to look at him. "I mean, the crazed machete-wielding maniac was scary as hell...but the way you guys took him down. It was like watching a Marvel movie."

"You're the devil's emissary! Charlene is right! You eat souls with your talons!"

The sound of sirens drew closer. Declan and Gavin looked at each other and said, "Charlene?"

Gavin yelled, "Frank!"

"Yeah," said a worker from inside the bay.

"Charlene Childress?"

Frank removed his Cummings and Ryan Grocery baseball cap and stepped out beside them.

"She was questioned and released," he replied.

"Any connection te dis eegit?" Declan asked.

"Charles Thomas Petersen? I believe Ms. Childress went to school with his father. I'm unaware of any other connection, but I'll get Captain Talbert on it."

"Take jurisdiction," Gavin commanded. "And take him to Quantico."

"Do you want to question him?" Frank asked.

"No. You and Gil can handle it," Gavin said. Then he looked at Declan.

"Aye. Alright. Uncail Eamon!" he called out.

"Aye," responded a man, younger than Frank but older than Declan and Gavin. He was balding, overweight, and clearly uncomfortable in the Virginia heat, as he was sweating profusely. He, too, removed a store baseball cap and stepped out of the workforce on the bay.

"Go wid Frank," Declan commanded.

"Uncle?" asked John, standing with Randy inside the bay.

"Aye, he's ma stepmother's younger brother."

"You guys aren't former military, are you?" John observed more than asked.

"Active-duty military intelligence," Gavin confirmed, patting the older man on the shoulder.

"So cool!" Todd chuckled.

CHAPTER 34

"What de ye mean, Eamon's a Captain in J2?" Merida yelled at her son. She sat majestically in a Laura Ashley armchair in the brightly lit living room, catty-corner to the sofa across from the white-painted brick fireplace. Her demeanor and posture were regal, her feet crossed at the ankles and tucked behind her knees and to her left side, her hands folded in her lap.

"Why're ye yellin' at me? I did na recruit 'im. It was de other way 'round!" Declan said to his stepmother.

"My brother? The boy I all but raised on ma own? He recruited ma child into a life of lies?"

"Jesus," Declan replied, unsure how to react.

"Mary and Joseph," Gavin quipped.

"More likely as not 'twas him," she argued, pointing at Gavin. "Ye always did whatever he did."

"I did na even know he was CID, but I 'ave been workin' wid Eaman for ten years."

"And I didn't know he was J2 until he walked into the middle of an ATF op, and members of the Bratva faction I had dismantled in December surfaced in connection with Declan's investigation into the Brotherhood," Gavin interrupted.

"What on Earth does ATF have to do with any of this?" John jumped into the conversation.

"The Bowens…Bowen Tobacco. A major Tobacco company cozying up to a radical Islamic group and Bratva…Theo was engaged to Igor Popov," Mary said.

"How would you know what ATF is investigating?" her mother asked.

Mary opened her mouth, but nothing came out. She sat

between Gavin on her right and Declan on her left on the sofa. She opened her purse, pulled out her credentials, and laid them on the coffee table in front of her.

"Mary, you're an ATF agent?" Meghan asked.

"Oh, Lord, no. I'm an analyst. Mr. Fox was the ATF agent. But he wanted me to work with him because Theo's my cousin. It gave me insight into her," she replied.

"I still do na see how ye got yer uncail involved. Gavin did na get his uncail involved," Merida insisted.

"Ma, Frank *is* Deb's uncail," Declan said indignantly. It wasn't Gavin's 'fault' that he was J2, but he obviously did have family involved, too.

"Ye take care, doncha, Dec? Ye do na let harm befall him?" his stepmother beseeched him, grabbing his arm.

"We take care o' each other," he answered after a moment's silence. Eamon had been a sickly child. Apparently, his stepmother, ten years older than her brother, still saw him as that little boy.

Dan, standing in the doorway, stepped forward. "Mrs. Mahoney, believe me, Gavin and Declan live by a code. Sometimes it's hard to see it. Sometimes it's hard to understand. But they'd never harm someone they love. Sometimes, they have to do things we can't accept easily. Last summer, Gavin revealed that I had a brother. He told me my brother had died 8 years before in a car accident. He told me that Sean Bowen, one of Theo's stepsons, had assumed my brother's identity to escape his father and identical twin brother, Kris. Kris was truly an evil man. He raped my wife in college. He killed Deb's mother. He kidnapped Jason. And in the end, he came for all of us. Mr. Davis shot him dead. That's when Gavin arrested Theo and Ivan Polaski. Then, last year, Sean Bowen showed up. Gavin knew that Sean wasn't Sean. He knew that he was Gil all along, but he had set up the cover, and they had been working on it for 8 years. He let me believe my brother was dead and that Sean wasn't. I've been angry at him ever since. But he did it to catch a much bigger fish. By keeping Gil undercover as Sean, they dismantled the Chicagoland faction of Bratva and uncovered a major infiltration into the US military by Bratva. The thing that hurt most was… I can't help but remember how he acted shocked that Sean was in that picture…how he pretended that he had seen someone he thought was dead. But I've come to realize…I…"

Gavin looked away and down. It was his tell. Declan had seen it his entire life. And he was sure Dan saw it too when he paused. Suddenly, Dan knew. Declan could see it in both their faces. Gavin hadn't been acting. And that wasn't Gil in that picture.

"My point is, they protect each other and their loved ones. And I am honored to be counted in that number," Dan said.

"Dani wants more ice cream!" Randy announced, skipping into the living room.

"I got it," Declan said, taking the opportunity to escape. He took Randy's hand and went to the kitchen, getting two bowls of ice cream. He handed one to Randy and carried the other upstairs to Dani, Randy trailing behind him.

He opened the bedroom door and asked, "How's my garl?"

The little girl smiled weakly. "My throat reawy huwts, Daddy," she said, looking up at him with huge violet eyes.

"Does it now? Let me see. Open," he said, moving to her bedside. He took a look at her poor, inflamed throat and felt her forehead. Still no fever. That was good. "Aye, ma darlin', yer throat is still very red, but ye have no fever. If ye want ice chips, ye can ''ave some of dem, too. And ye can take some Advil if ye like."

She shook her head. He laughed. He remembered avoiding medicine as a child. As she didn't have a fever, he wouldn't force her, even though it might help with her discomfort.

"How would ye like it if I lay wid ye fer a while? Ye too, Randy."

"Would yous sing that pwetty song?" she asked.

"I will indeed," he said, realizing the mournful feelings he usually experienced when he sang that song were gone with Dani's repeated requests for it. That simplistic happiness had replaced the grief in just a few hours.

He climbed into the middle of the bed with a small child on each side. He gave Dani her ice cream. He sang. And soon, all three were sound asleep.

He felt an overwhelming sense of peace, and he opened his eyes. He was sitting in the gazebo at the Davis home, behind the garage. A man sat on the bench next to him. He had red hair, like Uncail Daithi, Aintin Connie, and Miranda…and Dani and Randy. A sprinkling of freckles bridged his nose. His eyes were a deep violet-blue. He rocked his torso back and forth as he sat there.

"Hi, Declan," he said, looking straight ahead as if purposely avoiding looking at Declan.

"'Ello, Mike," Declan replied. "Why am I here?"

"It's my favorite place. It's where I told Mary I loved her, and she didn't laugh at me. She held my hand instead. Then she kissed me. It wasn't like with Deb, who did it on accident because I moved. And it wasn't like with Vanessa, who did it on purpose, but only because she wanted to control me. It was because she really cared about me. She really loved me."

"Aye, she wouldn't kiss ye if she didn't mean it. She's not dat kind. I know she loved ye. She's told me," Declan said, putting his hand on Mike's shoulder. "Ye're solid. I 'alf expected to not be able te touch ye."

"Yes. I'm real enough here," Mike said. He slowly stopped rocking. "I don't need the stims here. But I use them so people know me. Is it okay with you if I don't stim?"

"Aye, whatever makes ye feel natural."

"I like Gavin," Mike said.

"I do, too," Declan affirmed.

"I wasn't sure I liked you," Mike confessed.

"I understand. I can be a right bastard," Declan laughed. "Plus, I took yer garl."

Mike laughed. It was a good, natural laugh, not at all mechanical, the way it had "felt" before. "She saw you, and she was yours. I was jealous. You struck me as an insufferable flirt and a playboy. You lacked substance. You weren't good enough for her to look at you like that."

"Wow. I do na even know how te respond te dat. I'm a flirt, te be sure. I enjoy da company of a pretty woman. And until I heard her voice, I never fell. Playboy is fair, I suppose. But do I lack substance? Am I dat bad? And ye were jealous of me? I'm jealous of ye, after all. I've never been in love with anyone but Mary. She was in love with ye."

"You know, when I brushed your shoulder the first time, I felt the tattoo. I felt what it symbolized, why it was there. I went to find Kathleen, and she told me about who you really are. She showed me a scared boy no more than a child himself, who loved so well and so deeply that his heart kept her clinging to her life for 7 days. She showed me the tears you shed, the heartbreak you felt when she had no fight left. And she showed me the man who funded the NICU at hospitals around the world. She showed me the man you hid under that superficial shell," Mike continued. "You're a good man. Don't pretend to not be."

Declan felt the tears rolling down his cheeks. He sniffed. He shook his head. "I miss her, Mike. I would have given her da world."

"She stayed longer than she should have because you loved her so much. And now, you love them. You are right,

Declan. Mary loved me. But she was made to be yours. Mary was never intended to be mine for more than a moment. But you are right about more than that. Together, we can be the fathers we can't be alone. Kathleen isn't alone anymore. And my children have a father. I entrust my family to you. Keep me in my children's hearts. And they'll make room for you there as well," Mike finished.

******

When Declan hadn't returned after half an hour, Mary went looking for him. She found him lying on his back, his arms around the twins, each using him as a pillow. Dani was curled up against him, sucking her thumb, her head on his chest. Randy was turned away from him but hugging his arm, the one with the tattoo, his head resting on Declan's shoulder. All three were asleep. She smiled and grabbed his sock foot. "Declan," she whispered.

"Hmmmmm?" he said, rousing. "Oh, I fell asleep. Sorry, ma Lovely." He looked from one sleeping redhead to the next. "How exactly do I get out of dis?"

"Carefully," she whispered. She moved to the side of the bed and gently lifted Dani off him. With his arm free, he moved Randy and scooted down so that he could get out from between them. He put his arms around Mary and kissed her cheek.

Mary led him out of the bedroom and closed the door behind them. As she took a step toward the stairway, he grabbed her hand, pulling her back. "Whose will ye be in da hereafter?"

The question caught her off guard. She flung her arms around his neck and kissed him. "Yours," she answered, knowing it was true. There was no wall between her and Declan. There was no sense of impending doom…no regret…and there was joyous abandon. There was life. She'd always love Mike. He'd been a beautiful soul: smart, funny, quirky. But there had never been a future with him in it. She'd allowed him into her heart, but now she understood he had not owned it. Declan, on the other hand, owned not only her heart but the whole of her being. Where there had been no future with Mike, there was no future without Declan.

He pulled her into his arms and held her. She never wanted the embrace to end. But end it did when her mother called out to them that the Indy 500 was starting.

"Would ye like a Guiness...or dat soft drink yer dad calls beer?" Declan asked her.

"I'll have the Guiness if you are," she said. When he was halfway down the stairs, she said, "Declan, there's no need to be jealous. He's gone."

He stopped. "Is he, now? He told ye he loved ye in the gazebo out behind da garage at his parents' house. You kissed him dere. Ye were da third woman he ever kissed. Da first was Deb, and it was an accident. Da second was Vanessa, who used it te manipulate him, and da third was ye, whom he loved." Having finished speaking, he stuck his hands in his pockets and continued down the stairs and out to the porch, where the kegs were set up.

Deb was standing at the bottom of the stairs just inside the dining room doorway. She looked up at Mary. Mary felt gobsmacked. Deb said, "Mike is awful chatty about that kiss."

Mary followed Declan out onto the porch. He handed her a cup full of Guiness. He poured out his own before he spoke again. "I'm sorry, Mary. I'm having a shite day."

She set her beer on the porch railing and took his from him, setting it beside hers. "I'll race ya," she said, eyeing the beers.

"Are ye loolah?" he asked.

"Are ya chicken?" she retorted.

"Gavin, kin ye come be witness?" he called.

Gavin, Deb, Dan, and Miranda came out onto the porch.

"Mary, I'm Irish," he laughed.

"Declan, Honey, one grandparent was Irish, and the other three made moonshine. Your "shite" day is about to get worse. Because your wife is going to down that Guiness faster than you down yours," she replied smugly.

Gavin counted down. They each picked up their Guiness. Mary chugged the Guiness down and set down her empty cup while Declan had half left.

"Holy shite!" he exclaimed, laughing.

"Oh...Dude, she destroyed you," Gavin chuckled.

"Aye, I am humbled," he said, kissing her, "and utterly emasculated."

"Feel better?" she asked.

"Aye, oddly enough," he laughed, finishing his beer.

It was short-lived, though, as Captain Petersen drove up the driveway at a breakneck speed, slammed his pick-up into park, and emerged red-faced and disheveled from behind the steering wheel. He left the door open as he barreled toward the group on the front porch. "Where is my son?" he bellowed.

"Possibly on his way to Gitmo if he doesn't have the right answers," Gavin said, standing to his full height. "Stand down, Captain."

"Is this because he questioned your credentials?" the Captain stammered.

"Na. 'Tis because, in his drug-induced rant, he said a name dat implicated him in an ongoin' joint investigation into a credible threat of terrorist activity."

"Under whose authority did you detain him?"

"Immediately, under mine. Ultimately, under POTUS," Gavin said. "You've been drinking. Go home. If he's not involved, he'll be turned over to local authorities."

"For what?" screamed Emmitt Petersen.

"Assault with a deadly weapon, for starters," Gavin replied. "Not to mention the drug charges."

Emmitt made a move toward Gavin. Declan grabbed his arm and twisted it behind his back, bringing the Desert Storm veteran to his knees.

"Assault! You assaulted me!" he screamed.

"Give me a break," Declan scoffed. "Had I assaulted ye, ye'd know it."

CHAPTER 35

After the third cup of coffee, Emmitt Petersen was a little more affable. "I apologize. I don't know what I was thinking. Chaz needs help. He's an adult, but he's still my son."

"How well do you know Charlene Childress?" Gavin asked, sitting across from him. Declan knew his cousin well enough to let him ask the questions. People opened up to Gavin for some reason. It was really uncanny.

"Charlene? I went to college with her. I hadn't seen her in years. Strange, you should mention her. I ran into her a few months ago. Chaz and I took his kids to the Smithsonian. She was at the Egyptian exhibit…she introduced us to the curator…and one of the archaeologists…a Dr. Sabah…something. Chaz chatted the doctor up. He asked her out. She said she was engaged, but I got the feeling she was interested," Emmitt said, taking a sip of coffee.

"Do you know of any connection between Max James and Charlene Childress?" Gavin asked. There was no inflection. His voice was monotone, hypnotic. He rubbed his index finger slowly against his thumb. Declan chuckled. Gavin smiled. Dan looked back and forth between the cousins, apparently catching on that there was unspoken communication between them. Declan shook his head at Dan and held a finger to his lip, telling Dan to hold his tongue.

Emmitt, however, remained oblivious. He just watched Gavin's fingers. "Max James. She's Charlene's stepsister. Charlene's father is Fedor Popov. At least, that's what Chaz told me. I never knew her name to be anything other than Childress."

Gavin patted the man on the shoulder, rose, and walked

out of the room. Dan followed him, and Declan followed them both. They made their way out to the porch.

"And in da end, it's just a parlor trick," Declan laughed.

"Of course, it is. I don't have superpowers," Gavin laughed, lighting a cigarette. "Want one?" he asked, offering his cousin the pack. Declan took one and accepted the light Gavin offered.

"I do na know about dat. Ye're subtle about it. Dey do na see it 'appenin'," Declan said with a wry smile.

Dan looked perplexed, but slowly, daylight dawned. He shoved his friend's shoulder. "Hypnosis? Really?" he exclaimed, shaking his head.

Gavin laughed. Declan liked the camaraderie these two men shared. Over the last few days, whatever had angered Dan had seemed to have been resolved, and their friendship had returned. Declan could clearly see that Gavin loved the man like a brother. And Dan clearly idolized Gavin, but even more, he genuinely loved him back.

"Took you long enough. You'd still be wondering if Declan didn't start laughing like a jerk."

"Well, you guys are smarter than me," Dan announced.

"Ha! Dat's a load. I jest do na look at him through rose-colored glasses," Declan laughed.

"I'll call BS on that, Dec. You absolutely look at him through rose-colored glasses. We all do. I think you see through him because you are so like him," Dan said, shaking his head and laughing. He paused a moment. "Wait. I've spilled my guts to you before. Did you…"

"When?" Gavin scoffed.

"When you asked for the green light to date my ex," Dan said poignantly.

"God, no. I kinda wanted you to shut up," Gavin laughed.

"Oh. Good. So did I, truth be told. But I just kept talking…"

he replied.

"So dat shite aside, is da Captain in dere bein' truthful?" Declan asked.

"He was under. It's the truth as he sees it," Gavin said.

"Mary, Darlin'!" Declan called, "Kin ye come out here, please?"

Mary came out the door. Her face just made Declan want to smile. It happened every time he looked at it. So, he smiled. "What de ye know of Charlene's history?"

"Charlene Childress? She's originally from the Richmond area, I believe. She's never been married. She attended Randolph-Macon College in the late 80s. As far as I know, it's always just been her and her mother. She'd talk about growing up with a single mom. I think her mom's name is Deidre."

"She's English?" Declan asked. That explained a lot, he thought.

"I've never met the woman, Hon," Mary explained.

Gavin lowered the register of his voice and flicked his lighter, holding up the flame.

"Think, Mary. Any details you may know could be important. Any thing you've seen or heard…anything…no matter how inconsequential," Gavin said.

"She did attend the Christmas Party. Yes, I'd say the accent was English." Declan took a drag off his cigarette. Mary cocked her head. "While I wasn't given the pleasure of an introduction, she was talking to Howard about his cigarette. She said she worked for 40 years at Bowen Tobacco."

Declan scowled and snapped his finger in front of Mary's face. "Hey!" he exclaimed.

"What?" Mary asked, wide-eyed.

Declan pointed at Gavin. "Do dat agin, and I'll kick your arse," he declared.

"Do what?" Mary asked.

"You can try," Gavin chuckled.

"No. Seriously, dat's not cool," Declan replied.

"Okay. I'll ask first," Gavin agreed. "Promise."

"Oh...I want that promise, too," Dan said, raising his hand.

"What are you talking about?" Mary asked.

******

Mary slammed the bathroom door behind her. "I'm sorry, Mary. I should have asked first," Gavin called from the bottom of the steps.

"Should have asked what?" Deb's voice echoed from the dining room.

"Um...I kinda hypnotized her," Gavin replied. "Ow!"

His wife had apparently smacked him. Good, she thought. He hadn't asked anything embarrassing or made her do anything. He'd simply probed her memory for details about Charlene's mother. But it was humiliating. She'd forgive him. But right at this moment, she was seething. She checked her reflection. Her cheeks were red. She turned on the faucet and splashed cold water on her face, patting it dry.

There was a soft knock on the bathroom door. "Mary, Darlin', are ye alright?" Declan called from the other side of the door. "Do ye want me to deck 'im? He said he'll even let me."

She laughed. She opened the door and fell into his arms, wrapping her arms around his neck and pressing her cheek to his. "No. He was just showing off. It's a pretty neat trick when it isn't you it's being done to. But it's nice to know you'd punch your favorite person on the planet for me."

"Mary, ye're my favorite person on the planet," he affirmed, kissing her face.

"Okay...second favorite," she chuckled. "Recently downgraded." And maybe that was why Gavin had done it, she thought. Well, maybe one of the reasons.

******

Gavin found a secluded spot in the backyard under a giant oak tree. He cleared a spot and cleared the debris. He sat on the ground with his back against the tree, looking up at the leaves dancing in the warm breeze. He felt like total crap. He couldn't explain why he'd done what he'd just done. He was always careful not to pull that on his family and friends.

He didn't look at her as she sat down beside him. "I'm sorry, Mary. I really am. I don't know why I did that," he said. When was the funny going to start? Everything should be funny by now. While the headache had faded, his mood had only become gloomier. He was beginning to wonder if the marijuana was defective.

"I can think of at least 3 reasons you did it," she said.

"Really? Enlighten me," he said, adjusting his back against the tree trunk.

"Well, one: you didn't know I was alive," she said astutely.

He laughed. "As much as I hate it, I am rather used to being aware of that sort of thing. I don't like feeling ignorant."

"I know. And while I am not the one who perpetrated that particular ruse on you, it challenged your sense of control. Hypnotizing me gave you some of that back."

"Plausible hypothesis," he agreed. "And two?"

"Two, you're jealous," Mary proposed.

"I'm jealous? Of?" Gavin queried.

"Me," she replied, picking a dandelion.

"Why would I be jealous of you?" he sighed.

She picked several more dandelions. "Because I took one of the people you love the most and shifted the limelight, he shines on you a little to the right. He's one of the few people who is on equal footing with you. You want to be happy for him, and you are…just not completely." She started to weave the dandelions together into a wreath.

"Hmmm. That hadn't occurred to me. It's unlikely. I don't think I'm that petty."

"Gavin, everybody is that petty," she said.

"I'll stipulate that it isn't completely impossible," he acquiesced. "Three?"

"Three. You don't like me," she proclaimed.

"I like you, Mary," he retorted.

"No. You're trying to, but you don't. Everything about me reminds you of Shannon. My dark hair, my brown eyes, the fact that I took those kids and hid them from their family, your family." She turned to face him and put the dandelion wreath on her head. She'd been witness to the wreckage Shannon had left behind when they had split nearly 8 years ago. Mary was astute. It was clear Hal was Gavin's son. His age clearly led to Shannon having been the boy's mother. Declan had filled in the gaps, how Shannon had hidden Hal from Gavin for 6 years. "What we did was unforgivable, Gavin. It's okay not to like me because of it. In my own defense, I wasn't being malicious. I was sad. But it doesn't change what I did."

Gavin's lip quivered. "I don't know how to get past it, Mary. She took away my chance at bonding. She took away his first laugh, his first steps, his first word. It wasn't fair. And then, at the same time, she gave me everything I have. Because had she not hidden him from me, I'd have married her, and I wouldn't have Deb, and Jason, and my Essie. And I am so conflicted and angry and...hurt. I am trying to remember that you are not her, but you're right." He sobbed.

"I'm so sorry. I hope someday you can get past it. Maybe we just need time. But I'm not going anywhere. And neither are you. So, we'll just have to live with it until it's okay." She shrugged. "Does Hal see his mother's family much?"

"Yeah. Linda, Shannon's mom, raised him until he was 6. I can't just rip him away from her. Kyra, Shannon's sister, less so

I guess. She's an actress and has been doing some work overseas for the last 8 months or so. Before that, quite a bit. She badmouths me a lot, so I'm kinda happy she's not around so much. You're a smart woman, Mary. No wonder Howard recruited you. For the record…I do like you. But I'll work on my anger over the twins. Thanks. I needed to hear all of that," he said.

"I do want to ask you something, though," Mary said, resolutely. "Declan's mother. When…"

He looked at her and lit a cigarette. "September 11, 2001," he said, without waiting for the question. "North Tower. She was there for a finance meeting at Bank of America."

Mary stifled her tears. "Where was he?"

He smiled sadly, fighting his own tears. "Serendipity. With Uncail Aiden. Eating ice cream for breakfast."

Mary buried her face in her hands and let herself cry. "He was eating ice cream while his mother died in the North Tower?"

"Yeah. He's every bit as broken as I am, Mary. He just hides it better."

He wasn't going to get the giggles today. He was resigned to that.

CHAPTER 36

As evening approached, a generational divide occurred. Grandparents navigated to grandchildren, and the small group of cousins of Gavin, Declan, and Miranda, with their spouses, found themselves with more than enough willing babysitters. They decided to go out.

They made their way back to Colonial Beach and a seafood place called Drift near the Municipal Pier. "The town is nearly unrecognizable," Mary announced, taking a seat.

"What do you mean?" Dan asked.

"Hurricane Isabel tore up the town. Your houses were brand new because the houses that were there were destroyed. The Yacht Club, which had been brand new because of the fire, was destroyed again. The Municipal Pier was gone. All these buildings are…different…from when I was little. The mix of the new and the old here…it's unsettling. Even the Catholic Church. It's the same building…but it's unrecognizable from the building I was baptized in."

"Change is a constant," Gavin noted, paraphrasing The Big Bang Theory.

The waitress approached. "A bottle of yer best Irish Whiskey. And a glass wid ice," Declan said. "What will da rest of ye lot be 'avin'?"

Having given their order to the waitress, they sat around the table for a moment.

Deb grabbed Gavin's hand. He pulled it to his mouth and kissed it.

As the waitress returned with their drinks, Miranda quipped, "Well, we're a lively group."

Declan laughed. "Give me a minute te drink dis, and I'll give ye a show fer sure."

Eamon Riley approached the table. At 52, he had been married and divorced three times since 1996, when it had been legalized. He had three daughters of his own, two with his first wife, one with his third, and five stepdaughters between his second and third wives. He was only 14 years older than his nephew, but he looked 25 years older. He was bald, overweight, and had high blood pressure that manifested in a red complexion. He was also a good 5 inches shorter than Declan. None of this affected his competency. He was every bit as qualified and dangerous as his nephew. He grabbed Declan's bottle and took a giant swig.

"Help yerself dere, Uncail," Declan announced, holding up his finger to flag down the barmaid. Eamon handed the bottle to Frank, who appeared behind Dan. Dan yelped in surprise as Frank's hand came down on his shoulder.

"Jesus, Frank!" Dan said as Deb hid her smile behind her hand.

Frank likewise took a swig.

Frank, though twelve years Eamon's senior, looked 15 years younger. His hair was dark with a little salt and pepper at the temples. It was also full. He had been bald for a long time, shaving his head in solidarity with his brother, who had chronic leukemia. He had passed away a year and a half prior, leaving all his possessions to Gavin while the money, business, and properties had been divided among the family. Frank was also shorter than average but was trim and fit.

The two men pulled chairs from a neighboring table and joined the group as the barmaid brought the new bottle and two more glasses with ice. "Y'all eatin', too?" she asked. "Do you need menus?"

"Aye, I'm near starved," Eamon announced, winking at her.

"I could eat," Frank agreed.

She disappeared and reappeared with two more menus.

Mary took Declan's bottle, poured a glass for him, handed it to him, and asked, "Charlene Childress?"

Eamon looked at Declan. Declan nodded. "Charlene Childress was born in June 1968 in Henrico County to an unwed mother, Deidre Childress, an English ex-patriot living in da States. Her father is unknown but rumored te be Fedor Popov. Fedor and Boyd Bowen, adopted father of Walter Bowen, were close friends, and Deidre worked fer Boyd. Walter took over as CEO in 1995," Eamon explained.

"Wait, that old biddy really is Max's stepsister?" Mary asked. She was so disappointed. In Max, yes, but more so in herself for having believed Max. "How old is this, Fedor?"

"85. Vlad was born to his 6th wife when he was 55. Charlene and Vlad are his only two children. He appears to have struggled with fertility," Frank snorted.

"Sabah Al-Maghrabi was engaged to Vlad when she was killed," Mary continued.

"Yes," Gavin said contemplatively.

"What about Chaz?" Mary asked.

"His tox screen came back positive for methamphetamine. He's not a professional. Obviously, given the haphazard way he came at Gavin. Nor does he have any direct relationship with the Brotherhood or any other terrorist organization. His connection to Bratva is tenuous at best. We turned him over to local authorities after questioning him," Frank explained. "Miss James as well. I daresay they'll be out within a few hours."

"Get Chaz a spot in a good rehab facility," Gavin commanded. "His father is a decorated veteran. He deserves that much."

Frank smiled. "I already arranged it. I thought that would be the way you'd want to handle it."

"Thanks, Frank," Gavin said, looking at the ground.

More and more, Mary saw Mike in Gavin, not in his appearance. Gavin looked Mexican and clearly resembled his mother, who was a gorgeous woman in her own right. But there was a touch of Seamus in his appearance, too. Mike had looked like his maternal grandmother, Sarah Southerland, born Maeve Connelly. Declan looked more like Gavin than Mike had. But there was something. The lack of eye contact, his mannerisms, the way Gavin conversed…there she saw and heard Mike. Gavin clearly wasn't on the autism spectrum, but there was something about him. Mary couldn't help herself. She chuckled.

Gavin furrowed his brow and asked, "What's so funny?"

"When I met Declan, I couldn't figure out who it was he reminded me of…until he stood up when I did. That's when I realized it was you. And sitting here just now, I realize you remind me of…"

"Mike," Miranda interjected with a smile.

"I don't see it," Dan laughed, "but she does say it all of the time."

"I totally see it," Deb agreed with a stunning smile. "Besides Gavin and Mike, who do you know to use words like…"

"Hypothesis," Mary supplied.

"Right….to use words like 'hypothesis' in casual conversation?" Deb finished.

"Declan," everybody at the table answered.

Mary smiled coyly. "What's your IQ, Gavin?"

"Depending on the test, between 140 and 160," he answered nonchalantly.

"So was Mike's," Miranda offered.

"So is Declan's," Mary concluded.

Declan finished his bottle before he started to feel it at all. But then he felt it all at once. He could hear his words start to slur, and the room felt like it was moving around him. He pulled out his platinum card and held it up. "A pint fer everyone," he called out. He stood and swayed. "'Tis ma anniversary tammara. I'll be married a full week. In case da accent does na give it away, I'm Irish. 'Tis in our blood to drink...and sing...especially when we drink. So, I'm goin' to buy a round, and den I'm goin' to sing a drinkin' song. When I sing "Good luck to the Barley Mow," ye lot cheers 'Good luck' and drink...but just the first time each verse or ye'll run out afore I finish." He sang *The Barley Mow,* and by the end of the song, he had the entire bar in a great mood. Then he and Gavin sang *Peggy Gordon* together, followed by *Ride On.* The more they sang, the more they drank. Finally, Declan sang *Red is the Rose.*

Mary got chills again. His voice was haunting.

"Ye see, it only takes one and a 'alf Irishmen te turn any bar into an Irish pub," Declan announced, staggering as Mary slipped her arm around his waist to steady him.

"What? Eamon doesn't count?" she asked.

"Eamon did na sing," he said, nearly falling.

"Aye, because I did na drink dat much," Eamon said, helping Mary steady him on his other side. They started walking him toward the door.

"You need help, Deb?" Dan asked.

Gavin, his head down on the table, opened his eyes and smiled at his wife. "You're so bea...beautiful," he stammered.

"Please," she laughed.

With Deb on one side and Dan on the other, they got Gavin up and moving toward the door. Frank offered his arm to Miranda. She took it, and they followed them out to the limo.

CHAPTER 37

Mary helped Declan upstairs and to bed. "You'll pay for this tomorrow," she grunted, trying to pull off his boots. Camden boots, she noted. They were expensive and of high quality. What's more, he had several pairs. "You're a bigger shoe horse than I am."

"Ye ca…n 'ave all da shoe…s ye wan…t, ma darlin'. Dere's more money dan any one person has a right te in ma account…s. Take all ye want," he said, slurring his words and waving his hands wildly in the air.

She dropped the boots to the floor and crawled across the bed to look down at his face, taking his hands and pushing them down to either side of his head on the pillow. "I know you're drunk, but you should call the lawyer and tell him to file the postnup," she said, kissing his mouth.

"Over ma dead body," he said without even a hint of a slur, pulling her down to him and kissing her.

"Faker!" she accused, slapping his chest.

"Hmmm. Sue me," he said with a smile, looking at her adoringly.

She snuggled down into the crook of his arm. "Declan," she said.

"Hmmm?" he responded, kissing her head.

"There's a song you sang tonight about a lost love. And there's a rose…" she started.

"*Red is the Rose.* It's an old Irish ballad," he answered.

"I've heard you sing that before," she said.

"I do na recall singin' it before dis evenin'," he said, yawning.

"Well, it wasn't within the last two weeks. It was a long time ago," Mary said. Declan opened his eyes and sat up. "I mean, it had to be you, right? Otherwise, it's just too weird. I mean, it's pretty weird if it was you, but it would be weirder if it weren't."

"What are ye on about?" he asked, shivering once.

"You know what I'm on about. Kathleen Orla's funeral," she replied, blinking at him innocently.

He jumped out of the bed and grabbed his laptop. He opened it and inserted the claddagh thumb drive on his keyring he pulled out his front jean pocket. He searched frantically through the pictures until he found the one he wanted. It was of a little girl waving back at him, ghostlike among the gravestones. She had brown hair, brown eyes, and doe-like lashes. She wore a pink tee shirt with a sparkling rainbow behind a galloping unicorn.

Declan looked from the picture to his wife and back to the picture.

"I..." Mary started, but he interrupted her with a passionate kiss on her mouth.

When he pulled away, he said, "The first words I heard ye say were, 'Dis is fer yer daughter,' to dat mother in the coffee shop dat mornin'. All I knew was dat I loved ye. Ye were dere fer me at ma lowest."

******

"You can knock it off now. Everybody's gone," Deb said, plopping into the armchair.

"Knock what off?" Gavin responded with a wry smile. "Damn, Dec can hold his liquor. He's a pretty good actor, too."

"And the point?" she laughed.

He smiled lovingly. "Just giving the misconception of weakness," he said, winking.

"The two of you aren't mad at each other at all?" Deb asked, exasperated. She could usually read Gavin's emotions fairly well.

"Oh, he was mad. As he should have been. I gave into temptation on that one. I shouldn't have done it, DeBella. She's astute, though. She nailed me on my motives...when I didn't even know why I'd done it. I kinda get the Mike thing. She was attracted to his intellect and character."

"And Declan?" she asked, crossing her legs.

"He has those, too," Gavin laughed.

"Hmmm," she said, biting her bottom lip. "And all that dark hair, those steely blue eyes, not to mention the muscles and a great ass, all wrapped around that accent."

Gavin glared at her, and she laughed.

"Mike looked like my dad. He was a good-looking guy," Gavin defended his deceased cousin.

"Yes, he was. He was just a little...awkward...and he was very sick at the time. A fact he used to his advantage," she noted.

"Are you accusing Mike of manipulation?" he chuckled.

"Take it from the girl who got tricked into kissing him," she said with a smile.

"He did do that," Gavin laughed.

They sat quietly for a moment. Deb had liked Mary immediately. Gavin called her "astute." From him, that was high praise. He valued the power of observation...and the analytical prowess to process what was observed. But Mary was naïve, too. Deb could see clearly how Mary could be manipulated. Like herself, Mary suffered with a slight inferiority complex. She *was* astute. But she lacked confidence in her abilities. And she longed for acceptance. More than anything, Mary wanted to be liked and secretly feared she wasn't. It was her Achille's heel. It was how people like Max fooled her. This made Deb instantly protective of Mary. Hence, the disapproving slap she'd given to the back of her husband's head when he'd messed with Mary this morning.

Deb uncrossed her legs and stood. She walked over to

stand in front of her husband and lay her hands on his shoulders. He put his hands on her hips and looked up at her. "I know you like her. I know Declan loves her. Now that I see what was pissing me off about her, I admit it isn't that big a deal. She is clearly NOT like Shannon. I'll give her a chance. I think I like her, too, if that helps," he said.

She hugged his head to her abdomen and played with his hair. "It does. I'm sorry that this whole situation is bringing up these feelings for you again. And I'll remind you; it's okay to be happy. Being happy doesn't make us guilty about the bad things that happened along the way to our happiness."

CHAPTER 38

Declan looked up at the house. Unlike the modern structure next door, Gavin's house was a traditional beach cottage built on stilts. It had a wrap-around porch and dormers protruding from the a-frame roof. The siding was a beachy, bleached-out gray. The trim was white. The door was a nautical, navy blue. The steps up to the porch were double-wide. It was a lovely house. Mary was right; the house had been built after the previous structure was destroyed by Hurricane Isabel.

Gavin opened the door and walked out onto the porch. Dani dropped Declan's hand and ran to Gavin. "Pwetty Mister! I's come to see you!" she exclaimed as she ran.

"We really must teach her te play hard te get," Declan mumbled, following the little girl up the steps.

Gavin ushered the new family inside. "Grand Da and your Ma and Dad get off okay?" Gavin asked, walking ahead of Declan.

"Aye, dere flight was at 8 am. They left at 3 dis mornin'," Declan responded. "Uncail Dave and Aintin Gabbie went home, too?"

"Yeah, Dad is working tonight. Breakfast?" Gavin asked, leading them into the kitchen. Dani tugged on his shirt, and he reached down and picked her up.

Deb was sitting at the kitchen table, an old Formica top with chromed aluminum legs, diner-style table. Essie was in her highchair. She had scrambled eggs and watermelon slices with no seeds on the tray. She had a Pebbles ponytail and was wearing a pink onesie.

"Good morning," Deb greeted them. Mary sat at the table,

and Randy climbed into her lap.

Essie looked up at Declan and batted her eyes. Then she held up a pudgy fist with watermelon in it, apparently offering it to Declan.

"Oh no, Starlight, dat's yers. Ye need te eat it," Declan said, winking and patting her cheek.

She popped it into her mouth and held out her arms to him. "Eccan...up," she said. Deb handed him a wipe, and he wiped the toddler's hands and face before picking her up. Essie grabbed his face and gave a raspberry kiss on his cheek.

Gavin mumbled, "We've gotta teach her to play hard to get."

Mary and Deb looked at each other and burst out laughing. Declan wasn't exactly sure what was so funny, but he had a feeling it was at his expense.

Gavin looked at Declan. "Wanna trade?"

"Ye give me ma kid, and I give ye yers?"

"Yeah," Gavin said.

"Sure," Declan agreed. He offered Essie to Gavin. Essie hugged his neck. "Wan Eccan," she giggled.

"I's want Pwetty Mister," Dani giggled, hugging Gavin.

"Dey're messin' wid us!" Declan laughed. "'Eccan' is pretty good. How many werds does she 'ave?" He gave her a tickle.

"Mama, Dada, Ha for Hal, Ay for Jason, wan, up...and Eccan, apparently," Gavin said, kicking at Declan's ankle.

"Watch de boots," Declan demanded. "De're costly."

"I know how much they cost. I'm wearing the same ones," Gavin pointed out, holding up one foot.

Declan looked over at the two women, who were looking at them both with a dumbstruck expression. "What?" he said.

"Nothing. Nothing at all," Mary said, holding up her hands. Deb just laughed.

From the beachside door, Miranda called, "Hello! Good morning."

Declan exited the kitchen. "Good mornin' te ye," he said, giving Essie a raspberry on the cheek in return for the one she'd given him. She giggled. "Ahhh. Sweet revenge," he teased as Gavin followed him out with Dani in his arms.

He gave Declan a playful shove. "I'll kick your ass once you put down my kid," he retorted, laughing.

"Ye can give it a whack," Declan said, kicking backwards at him.

Dan, behind Miranda, who had Sammy on her hip, blinked at them several times. "You two seem none the worse for the wear," he observed.

"Oh, we weren't drunk," Gavin said, grinning.

"Yeah, I got that when you winked at me when I carried you out," Dan laughed.

"I told you; I won't lie to you if I don't have to," Gavin promised.

"Daddy, my throat hurts," Dani complained, reaching for Declan.

"Does it now, Pixie? Starlight, go back te yer Daddy den."

Gavin set Dani down and took Essie. Declan picked up his stepdaughter and felt her forehead. "Let's take yer temperature. Ye might be a wee bit warm. Then ye can have some more Tylenol and some sorbet. Okay, ma garl?" The child nodded, pouting and hugging his neck.

He dug through the bag they'd brought to find the thermometer and Children's Tylenol and sat on the sofa with her. He aimed the thermometer at her forehead. It read 99.9 F. He gave her Tylenol. He hugged her to his chest and kissed the top of her head. Somehow, his fear had been replaced with cool assurance. And along the way, these two little angels had stolen his heart. "Daddy" wasn't just a name they called him. He had started to feel it and be it. Suddenly, "Daddy" was his identity.

Gavin set a bowl of sorbet on the coffee table and smiled. "It changes everything, doesn't it?" he said to Declan, who closed his eyes and nodded, hugging the daughter he now considered his own. Again, he felt the breeze on his shoulder. This time, it was warm and comforting.

CHAPTER 39

Despite Dani's sore throat, it was a great morning. Sam and Connie went over from Dan and Miranda's house to Gavin's shortly after Dan and Miranda. Sam had been making headway on gaining forgiveness for nearly driving Mary away from his wife. Connie had allowed him to share the bed last night. He'd spent the last week in a guest room. But after the previous evening spent with Dani and Randy, she'd been in a good mood. When they had come through the beachside door into the living room, and Randy had come running to her, calling "Granny!", Sam knew he was going to survive this debacle. She squeezed his hand, and her eyes twinkled when she smiled at him before kneeling to hug the child.

Sam had to admit he'd been wrong about Declan. Watching him interact with the children, Sam realized he was very kind and gentle. Sam winced every time they called him "daddy," but when he took out his phone and started showing the twins pictures of their father, Declan immediately stepped back so as not to intervene.

Further, Declan's relationship with Gavin was genuine and easy. More importantly, Gavin's relationship with Declan was genuine and easy. Sam trusted Gavin's judgment about people. He watched them throughout the morning. They acted like a couple of 13-year-old boys most of the time. Even Dan seemed to enjoy being around them together.

As morning slipped into the afternoon, Sam found himself preparing the grill on the deck of Gavin's house. Gavin was smoking a cigarette and playing Roy Orbison music over his outdoor speakers. Declan and Dan were sitting with him. All three seemed to be enjoying themselves.

Connie, the love of his life, glorious and beautiful, came out with the burgers to cook. She had on white shorts and an unbuttoned white dress shirt of Sam's over a black camisole. Her legs were long and graceful. She still made his heart skip a beat. She smiled at him as she stepped off the final step down from the porch to the deck.

It had been many months since Sam had begun to think of Gavin as a catlike creature, a sphinx. He explained it as being hyperaware. Dan, likewise, had outstanding reaction time in an emergency. Declan appeared to have that same sixth sense. Sam had seen it twice in two weeks already. So, when the three men jumped from their seated positions like three…cats jumping on a mouse, Sam immediately ducked.

Sam heard the gunshot after the men jumped, but before he saw the gunmen. Gavin hurled himself over the banister of the deck and dropped the 6 feet to the sidewalk below. Dan tackled Connie. Declan hurled himself at the grill, grabbing the metal spatula Sam planned to flip the burgers with.

He watched in stunned silence as Declan threw the spatula, like one would throw an ax, at the gunman. The sharp cleaver edge of the spatula designed for cutting into grilling meat to check doneness buried itself in the neck of the first assassin. Gavin, having circled in behind the two intruders, grabbed the second from behind and twisted the man's head, breaking his neck. Both assailants fell.

Dan, in a panic, jumped up and ran up the 4 steps from the deck to the wrap-around porch and into the house. Less than a few seconds later, he yelled out that everyone was alright and that the only casualty had been the antique Tiffany lamp Miranda had picked out for Deb when she'd been on bedrest while pregnant with Essie.

"Holy cow, you guys are fast!" Sam exclaimed, pulling

himself to a standing position.

"Not fast enough," Gavin said, holding his side. Then he held out his hand, revealing his palm covered in blood. A red stain quickly spread on his white shirt where his hand had been.

Declan, who had landed unscathed on the deck floor by the grill near Sam's feet, scrambled to stand and rushed to Gavin's side before he collapsed against Declan. Declan half carried Gavin back up the steps and helped him to a chaise lounge before calling for Dan for help.

Declan ripped Gavin's shirt to get a clearer view. "First aid kit!" he screamed.

"It's just a flesh wound," Gavin exclaimed. But he was grimacing in pain as he said it.

"Aye. Dat it is. I can see da bullet. Ye'll live. Jesus, ye scared da crap out of me," Declan said, collapsing to his knees beside the chaise lounge.

Connie sat up and held her arm. Sam rushed to her side. "Connie, Honey, are you hurt?"

"Just a few scrapes…and I can't move my arm," she said, fighting tears.

"Sit still, Aintin. I'll be right dere," Declan said, rising. He came over and knelt beside her. Sam looked at him. He saw a good man.

The sun was bright. Sam's eyes started to water. He blinked against the odd increasing light. Maybe he was having a stroke or another angina attack. But as he watched Declan tending to his love, a man's figure appeared in the light behind Declan. The man put a steadying hand on Declan's shoulder. Sam found it hard to breathe. Mike's face formed in the light.

"Call 911!" Dan yelled as he emerged from the house with the first aid kit.

Then, the light faded to black.

Sam regained consciousness to a bevy of activity. An

EMT stood over him. "Oh, there you are. Feeling better? You hyperventilated and passed out. Not that I blame you. This is some call," the man chuckled.

Sam sat up as two body bags were lifted off the beach below and carried between his daughter's house next door and Gavin's house. The Hogues, the couple who owned the house on the other side of Dan's and Miranda's house, stood on their dock watching the activity. He turned his head to look at the Dockside Restaurant just across the mouth of Monroe Bay to his left. The patio was full of people watching from that viewpoint. They were the center of attention.

Directly to his right, Deb was holding onto Gavin's hand for dear life. "Who dressed your wound? Nice job," the EMT tending to Gavin said.

"Declan. He was a medic. Also, he has an MD," Gavin said, nodding to his cousin, who sat nonchalantly on the deck banister with his back to the river. Mary stood leaning against him, his arms around her.

A third EMT, tending to Connie, said, "Yeah, I think your nephew is right. It was wise not to put your shoulder back in the socket. I think you have a broken clavicle. You'll need x-rays to confirm."

"Which one is the medic? The one who turned the cooking utensil into a deadly weapon, or the one who broke the guy's neck with one movement?" asked a police officer, standing in the middle of the deck with a pen and paper pad in his hands.

"That would be me...spatula," said Declan.

"And you tackled your mother-in-law?" the cop asked, pointing at Dan, who Sam realized was sitting in a chair behind him, with Miranda holding his hand, sitting in the chair next to him.

"Um, yes, sir," Dan replied.

The cop laughed. "I'd have volunteered to tackle my

mother-in-law," he said under his breath. Then louder, he inquired, "Are you like special ops, guys?"

"Special ops?" Gavin asked. "Ow," he said as the EMT repacked the wound.

"Yeah…like Delta Force or Green Berets or something?" the cop continued.

"No. I'm CFO of Fuentes International. I used to be a police officer. My cousin is an attorney. We both served in the armed forces. I was in the US Army. Declan in the Irish Army. Dan is a deputy sheriff in Kane County, Illinois."

"That correct, sir?" the cop asked, looking at Sam. Sam nodded. "And what do you do?"

"I…I'm also an attorney," Sam said, finding his voice. "Who were…they?" He nodded toward the beach.

"They were security personnel from a company called…" He checked his notes and laughed. "Delta Force Security, LLC. Now that's funny right there. Mercs?" He looked between Declan and Gavin.

"How would we know?" Declan asked, straight-faced.

"Alright then. Well, that's all I need, I guess. Don't go leavin' the state," he laughed again.

CHAPTER 40

Declan, Mary, Dan, Miranda, and the kids made their way into the Mason Dixon Café, just up the street from Mary Washington Hospital. "Wan Eccan! Wan Eccan," Essie screamed, struggling in Hal's arms. Poor Hal. He was a strapping lad for seven, but the flailing toddler was too much for him. Declan took Essie from his arms and winked at the boy.

"Sometimes, it's best te jest give up, lad," Declan told him.

Essie hugged Declan's neck as the hostess approached.

"Four adults and 60,000 children...no 6...6 children... two highchairs, please," Declan said with a charming smile. The waitress beamed. Mary smiled and rolled her eyes.

"Do you know how to interact with a woman without flirting?" Mary asked, taking his arm.

"I admit, I 'ave naever tried," he teased, kissing her cheek.

The hostess led them to a table. They all sat down.

"I's want chickens and fence fies," Randy announced.

"Daddy, my throat still hurts," Dani said, tugging on Declan's sleeve.

"Alright den, Pixie. We'll see what dey 'ave dat won't hurt so much. How about da bread pudding? Aye? And dat sounds good, Randy. How about ye, Hal?" Declan asked.

Hal looked through the menu and ordered a salad with oil and vinegar on the side.

Dan laughed. "Your dad isn't here, Hal. It's okay to eat kid food."

Miranda elbowed him in the ribs.

Declan concurred. He leaned forward and said, "I will na tell 'im. Get what ye really want."

Hal looked around and then whispered, "Can I have macaroni and cheese?"

"Kin ye 'ave mac-n-cheese? O' course ye kin. What kind of question is dat? Mac-n-cheese fer da boy," Declan said, smacking the table. "And I'll have the Veggie, no mayo, and dat salad he does na want," he whispered loudly behind his hand, making Hal and Jason laugh.

Mary laughed, too. "He only eats fish, chicken, and vegetables and very few carbs. Next to no fat and only a little sugar."

"No kidding. Gavin eats the same way," Dan interjected.

"A pancake for the baby, and I'll have cheeseburger and fries," Mary added.

"Pancake and cheeseburger and fries work for me, too," Miranda said. "How about you, Jason?"

"Hot dog, please," Jason ordered.

"The Mureca Burger," Dan ordered. "I plan on getting fat and happy."

"Aye, eat like dat, and ye will," Declan teased. "Sooner dan later." Now that he knew Gavin was okay, he was in a good mood. His wife and kids were okay. He had another connection between Bowen Tobacco, Bratva, and the Brotherhood: Delta Force Security, LLC.

Declan noticed the man and young woman across the restaurant. When he had banged on the table, it had drawn their attention. They argued quietly. The man lost as the woman jumped up and rushed over. She snatched Essie out of the highchair and yelled, "Hal! Jason! Go to Rudy now!"

Dan and Miranda, whose backs were to the couple, started laughing. "Chill out, Katelynn. They haven't been kidnapped," Dan commanded.

Katelynn, whoever she was, turned dumbstruck to face the deputy. "Dan...um...oh..." she stammered.

"Allow me to introduce Katelynn Kaminski, Declan. She's Deb's sister," Dan laughed. "Katelynn, this is Declan..."

"Mahoney. Oh crap. You're Gavin's cousin from Ireland. I'm so sorry. I...I didn't recognize...My niece and nephews were with someone I didn't know...I..." she continued.

"Katelynn, please. It's all good. Ye were just bein' protective of yer family," Declan said, smiling as he stood to shake her hand. Katelynn looked at him intently, holding onto his hand long after she should have let go. He winked.

Mary kicked his shin.

"Ow. My wife, Mary," he said, releasing Katelynn's hand.

The man cleared his throat. Katelynn continued to stare at Declan... kind of like Essie stared at him earlier. Dan shook his head and laughed heartily. "That's her boyfriend, Officer Rudy Vance, Fredericksburg PD."

"Nice to meet ye, Rudy. Gavin speaks highly of ye," Declan said, offering his hand to the man. Rudy looked at Katelynn, shook his head, and clasped Declan's hand.

Rudy elbowed his girlfriend. "That's his *wife*, Mary," he teased.

Declan looked at Mary and felt the smile vanish from his face. "Mary?"

Tears filled her eyes, and she stood and walked away.

"Excuse me," he said, and followed her out the door.

He caught up to her just outside the door. He grabbed her hand and pulled her to stop. She turned and started hitting his chest. He pulled her to him and hugged her until she stopped fighting him and her arms wrapped around his neck, and she just cried.

"What is it, ma darlin'?" he asked, holding her tightly against him.

"A few hours ago, there were people shooting at you. Last week, you were stabbed while fighting off multiple assailants.

And now you're casually flirting with other women…and I don't know how to live like this," she cried.

Declan lifted Mary's face with his hand under her chin. "Look at me, ma Lovely. I do na want ye te live dis life. I do na want te live dis life anymore. But we're in it right now. Dere's only one way out. Will ye trust me? Do ye trust me?" He searched her eyes for the truth. He wiped her tears from her cheek with his thumb. She sighed, and the fear in her eyes faded a little. "I'm sorry I flirted. But it was only a flirtation. Ye're da only one I want. I swear."

She nodded. "It's who you are. You're a flirt. It's part of your charm. I just really prefer it when you flirt with me."

"Aye, I'll keep dat in mind, ma darlin'," he said, flashing that smile. He leaned in and kissed her, his hand still under her chin.

CHAPTER 41

Rudy pulled up a chair across from Dan and watched Declan and Mary's interaction. "Spooky," he said.

"What's spooky? Gavin's cousin? How he's exactly like him? You don't even know the half of it," Dan retorted.

"They're not exactly alike," Miranda noted. "Gavin pretends he doesn't know he's sexy as hell. Declan makes no such pretense."

"They're your cousins, Sweetheart," Dan teased his wife.

"You fall somewhere in between the two of them," Miranda said, giving him a quick kiss.

"I was commenting more on the...way they carry themselves, I guess...but it's something in their eyes...the intelligence...the awareness of their surroundings. He knew we were heading over here before I did," Rudy noted.

"Oh, that," Dan laughed. "It's all the same thing, Rudy. Declan is Gavin without all the bad crap that has happened to him...and with an Irish accent."

Rudy watched, amused, as Declan led Mary back inside and to the table. As a casual observer, he'd know Mary loved the man desperately. As Gavin's protégé, he recognized Declan loved her even more desperately, flirting aside. He'd seen that same look in Gavin's eyes. He pitied the man who might try to harm Mary Mahoney.

He understood love. The little spitfire with him, who had so blatantly ogled Declan moments before, had quickly become the center of his world after he'd met her. She was the inspiration behind the tattoo on his right forearm, a crystal ball in a female hand with her name in its center. He'd move heaven and earth for her.

They moved their table to join the group. Rudy asked, "So, Gavin okay?"

"Just a scratch," Declan answered.

"Was he the one that killed the guy with the spatula?" Rudy continued, taking a bite of his food.

The waitress arrived with their food.

"Na, dat was me. He broke de other one's neck," Declan responded coolly. Ever so cool. Just like Gavin.

The waitress nearly dropped the plate she set in front of him.

Rudy laughed and put his shield on the table. "It's alright. It was a home invasion. They're not criminals. The homeowner, his cousin, is our former head detective, in fact...the one who solved the songster serial killer case a year and a half ago."

"Oh...yeah," the wide-eyed waitress said.

As Declan ate, he changed the subject. "I like da tattoo, Rudy. Where'd ye get it?"

"You want a tattoo?" he asked, taking another bite.

"Aye, I think I do," Declan said.

"Alright, I'll take you," he agreed. He thought he might like this guy, but he wasn't sure yet.

"What are you doing, Dec?" Mary laughed.

"Hey, sounds like a plan," Dan interjected. "I've been thinking of getting one for a while."

"Count me in," came the voice from behind Rudy. He turned to find Gavin and Deb standing behind him. Sam and Connie were behind them.

"Granddaddy!" the red-headed little girl called. Hadn't she called Declan "daddy"?

Once they had all eaten, Rudy took the three men to the tattoo parlor while the rest went shopping, agreeing to meet them in 2 hours.

******

Tito, the shop's owner, looked at the two white men Rudy brought in and snickered. The Mexican was clean-cut, too, but he looked tough enough. But the white men were already in their thirties, and their skin was pristine. They had no clue what they were in for.

The Mexican's torso was well-defined but covered in scars, and there was a bandaged wound. "Uh, what happened?" Tito asked.

"I was shot," the Mexican answered.

He wanted a spider with a ruby on its back on the back of his shoulder. Tito had the web circle around the shoulder and down his arm. It was very cool looking.

The taller of the two white men, the American, wanted his wife's name down his side. He was also quite well-built and muscular. He surprisingly did not even flinch.

The other white man, the Irish guy, wanted a single rosebud with his wife's name scrolled around it over his heart. Surprisingly, he already had a cuff tattoo on his bicep. He also had a wound on his torso that was healing.

"Were you shot, too?" Tito asked nervously.

"Nope," he said coldly. "Stabbed."

After several minutes of silence with the only sound being the buzz of the tattoo needle, the Irishman said, "Ye do nice work. Igor Yanovich's Russian lion is quite good. So was the eagle on that guy's forearm dis morning."

"You know Igor?" Tito asked.

"Not really. I jest noticed da tattoo when he stabbed me," the Irishman said.

"Igor stabbed you?" Tito asked uncomfortably.

"Aye. Den, I shot him," the Irishman continued.

"Oh. Is he okay?" Tito asked, feeling even more uncomfortable.

"He's dead," the Irishman said coldly, dead eyes locked on Tito. Tito swallowed hard.

"And the guy this morning?" Tito asked.

"I threw a spatula at him, impaling it in his jugular. He bled out in seconds." It was the coldest thing Tito had ever heard anyone say, and it gave him chills. He didn't much care for Igor or Dimitri. Dimitri Yanovich was Igor's brother and the first person that came to mind when the Irishman had mentioned the eagle tattoo. But this guy was talking about their deaths like they weren't even people. It made Tito's blood run cold.

"Do ye know where they worked?" asked the Irishmen, but it wasn't a real question. Tito had a feeling he already knew the answer.

Tito cleared his throat. "A security company, I think. I don't know."

"Ye do know," the Irishman said just above a whisper.

"Delta Force Security," Tito answered, feeling threatened.

"And do ye know anyone else who works at Delta Force?" the Irishman whispered again, his eyes still cold. Tito understood he wasn't looking for just any employee. He wanted one that would talk, who wouldn't mind that he'd killed Igor and Dimitri.

"Marshall Craig. He's an ex-Marine. I'm doing a large dragon on his back."

The Irishman smiled and held up a business card. "Tell 'im te call me...tonight," he said.

"O...okay," Tito stammered.

******

"Well?" Gavin asked as Declan came out of the tattoo shop.

"Marshall Craig, ex-Marine," Declan replied.

"Got it. I'll get you his info within an hour," Gavin said, smiling and walking toward his wife and kids.

Declan headed toward his family.

Dan slapped Rudy on the back. "They're intense," he laughed.

"Uh, yeah. I'm glad I'm not Marshall Craig," Rudy chuckled. "Of course, this was about the shooting this morning. I should have known."

"Yep. You should have," Dan agreed. "See ya around, Rudy." Then Dan also walked toward his family.

Rudy waved and turned to Katelynn. "Hey, Babe," he said, putting his arm around her shoulders. God, she was cute.

CHAPTER 42

Mary tucked the children into their beds in her apartment. It had been a very long day. They were exhausted and confused about a lot of what had happened.

Declan had hugged and kissed them both good night. Randy, who had accepted him immediately, was so happy it was amazing. He wanted nothing more than a dad, and now he had Declan. Dani had been harder to convince. But within a few hours, Declan had won her over just by loving her. Mary had been blind to how badly they had been craving a father. She'd been so preoccupied with her own grief and then Dani's illness and finally keeping her well, she'd completely missed the signs.

She closed the door and turned off their light.

The third bedroom was meant to be Randy's room, but the twins had refused to sleep in separate rooms. Over the two years she'd been living in the apartment, it had become a storage room of sorts. Declan had cleaned it out their first evening back and moved his exercise equipment into it. She heard him in there now, the weights clanking as he used them. She stood in the doorway, watching him.

He didn't seem to notice her, so she stayed. His muscles rippled under the weight. His skin glistened with the effort he exerted. He was breathtaking. Literally. She found it hard to breathe looking at him. She took a step inside the door. His eyes were closed, but he smiled as he put down the weight and reached out, grabbed her hand, pulled her to him, and kissed her.

"Ew!" she squealed. "You're all sweaty."

He pressed her against the wall. "Aye, dat I am, but so will ye be afore I'm done wid ye," he said, nuzzling her ear. She had no words. She just exhaled her surrender and clung to him for dear life.

******

Declan let the hot water cascade down his face. He closed his eyes and let the shower rinse away the weekend along with the suds. He shut off the water and stepped out of the shower. He dried off and then dried his dark hair and slipped into jeans and a tee shirt. He leaned on the sink and stared at his own reflection. He barely recognized himself. He was smiling.

He walked into the bedroom. Mary sat on the bed, brushing out her long brown hair. She smiled at him. Before he could say anything, his phone on the nightstand rang. "I'm goin' out. I'll be back later," he told her, grabbing his shoes. He picked up his phone and carried it outside. As he closed the apartment door behind him, he answered it. "Yeah," he said, walking to his Mercedes.

"Hello, Declan," said the man's voice.

"Hey, dere, Gunny. So, ye're da man wid da dragon tattoo? I jest need to know what ye know about Delta Force Security," Declan replied.

"Time to take down DFS?" Gunny asked.

"Aye. And maybe we can prevent a terrorist attack before it 'appens. Who's behind DFS?"

"Not over the phone. Can we meet?" Gunny asked.

"Aye. J. Brian's Taproom on Hanover St. in Fredericksburg. 11 pm," Declan replied. "Bring me evidence."

******

Declan walked into the bar room, found a table in a dark corner, and took a seat. A barmaid came over and put a coaster on the table in front of him.

"I'll 'ave a Guiness, Vicky," he said.

"Do I know you?" Vicky asked.

"No. But yer boyfriend will be in lookin' fer me in a few

minutes. Bring him his regular Bud Light, such dat it is," he replied.

She looked at him incredulously but left and returned with both beers.

A minute later, Marshall "Gunny" Craig entered the bar room, smiled, and waved at his girlfriend, who nodded at Declan's table. He followed her gaze and slowly approached Declan, hidden in the shadows, who calmly took a sip of his Guiness and motioned for Marshall to take a seat. Marshall accepted the unspoken invitation and sat. "Okay, how are y... you, Dec?" he stuttered.

Declan smiled. "Fine." He leaned forward into the light.

Marshall turned a thumb drive slowly between his thumb and forefinger. "N...n...nice job stopping the b...bus b...b... bombing in Dublin in November." He smiled. "Took you long enough to catch up."

Declan smiled again.

Marshall sat the USB drive on the table and slid it toward Declan. "It's all th...there. Financials, m...m...memos, encrypted emails. It lays out the entire p...plan. When the Grand Egyptian opens in the fall, they will host every school in C...Cairo for a soft opening 'field trip.' The p...p..plan is to hijack and b...b...bomb every bus that is not from a B...Brotherhood school. It will be a major t...t...terrorist attack...on children."

Declan picked it up and held it up. Captain Talbert bumped him, and the USB drive disappeared. Marshall jumped in a panic. "Do na let the face scare ye, Gunny. He's neither Kris nor Sean Bowen. He's CID." Declan reassured his drinking partner, taking another sip. "He'll be takin' Vicky wid him when he leaves...te keep her safe. Will ye walk into the Lion's den wid me?"

"I'm a M...marine," Marshall replied proudly. "And you know I will."

"Good on ye. Tamarra. 9 am. Fox, Goodwin, and Kane.

Near the Marine Memorial in Arlington. I'll introduce ye," Declan said.

"To whom?" Marshall asked.

"Ye'll find out tamarra at 9 am." Declan chugged down his Guiness and stood to leave.

CHAPTER 43

Tuesday morning, Declan donned his fatigues. There were no more secrets in his life. He gave Dani her medicine and packed the kids into the car.

"Your red hat is funty, Daddy," Randy giggled as Declan buckled him into his booster seat.

"Is it now? What's so funny?" Declan asked, feigning indignation.

"It doesn't match the green shirt and pants," Randy giggled.

Declan smiled and caressed the boy's cheek. "Dis is da Irish armed forces uniform, and I wear it wid pride, ma son…red hat and all."

Mary came out of the apartment and headed toward them. She was breathtaking in a Chanel white pencil skirt that came just above her knees and a matching blazer. Under the blazer, she wore a white silk camisole top with lace trim. Her legs were bare and tanned to a pretty golden hew naturally by the sun. She wore a pair of simple white pumps. The outfit was elegant and simple. He'd ordered it for her, along with several other expensive outfits, on a whim right after he'd met her. He was blown away by the result.

"Wow," he said as she stopped in front of him and smiled.

"I can't believe how much this cost…but I have to admit, I make it look good," she quipped.

He winked at her. "Dat ye do, ma Lovely."

"You look pretty good there yourself, Major Mahoney," she said, admiring his appearance.

They dropped the kids off at daycare and headed to the

office.

He parked in his reserved spot, got out, and walked around to her door, which he opened for her. He offered her his arm, which she took. They took the elevator from the car park to the lobby of their building with Wade Hinson, an attorney in the firm, and Gail Jacobs, a clerical assistant. Mary knew they had been secretly dating, but they had been wary of making it known. As the elevator doors closed, she smiled and said, "What's the worst that can happen, Gail?"

Gail turned to look at the couple. Declan winked at her. Her face broke out in a huge grin, and she grabbed Wade's arm. He smiled and turned to face the doors, but he held a thumbs-up behind his back. Declan chuckled.

The four of them transferred to the building's main elevator. Gloria and Mr. Kane stepped into the elevator. "Hold, please," came a voice just as the doors started to close. Gavin, dressed in his fatigues with Deb on his arm, stepped inside. Colonel Walters, also in uniform, followed them on.

"We can recommend a great wedding chapel in Vegas, Gail," Mary said. "General Mahoney and Deb got married there, too. You liked the chapel, didn't you, Deb?"

"Oh, yes. It is a very pretty little chapel, and the service was excellent," Deb replied enthusiastically. "It's a small business, not a franchise."

"Mahoney?" Mr. Kane asked, turning to look at Gavin.

"I look like my mother," Gavin replied.

"No. I'm sorry, I meant…" Mr. Kane stammered, pointing at Declan.

"We're cousins. Our fathers are brothers," Declan explained. "He's two years older dan I am."

"Now, why do you have to go around telling people that?" Gavin asked, laughing.

"It explains the gap in rank," Declan teased.

"Except I was promoted to General 6 years ago," Gavin mumbled.

"Show off," Declan retorted and winked.

"Um…he hasn't asked me yet," Gail said after a moment's silence just before the elevator doors opened.

"You want me to ask you?" Wade asked, stepping off the elevator, still holding Gail's hand.

"Of course, I want you to. I love you, Wade," Gail confessed.

"You do? Really? I love you, too, Gail," Wade answered, kissing her hand as they walked side by side down that marble-tiled hallway.

"Wade is from Aurora, you know?" Mary said.

"So? What's that got to do with anything?" Gloria asked. Her tone was harsh, Declan noted.

"So, one of these two moguls is going to have to offer him a job after the shit hits the fan," Mary quipped.

Declan and Gavin burst out laughing.

******

Declan pushed open the door to his office at the end of the marble hall. Mary smiled as he walked through the doorway in front of her. Deb grabbed her arm and whispered, "I saw that."

"Hmmm. I was having visions of him lifting weights shirtless last night," she whispered back.

"Did he catch you watching him? That's always fun… when they catch you watching," Deb giggled.

"He did," Mary admitted.

Gavin sighed heavily. "Great. Yours isn't embarrassed by sex, either. We're doomed," he said, taking off his cap and throwing it down onto the desk.

Declan felt panic growing. He turned to his cousin. "They would na say dese things in public?"

"Wanna bet?" Gavin said, sitting on the sofa.

Deb practically purred as she sat on his lap and seductively wrapped her arms around Gavin's neck. "You once said you don't mind that I like sex," she whispered.

"Oh, I don't mind," he smiled back at her, a mischievous glint in his eyes. He put his arms around her and pulled her closer. "I rather enjoy being doomed." He kissed her neck.

"Do I need to be here?" Frank asked.

Deb climbed off Gavin and said, "Sorry, Uncle Frank." She laughed and caressed her uncle's shoulder. He shook his head.

Mary took Deb's arm. "Come on. Let's go get some coffee." She had quickly come to admire DeBella Mahoney. She had more grace and class than any of the women Mary worked with, certainly. More than that, she was one of the least judgmental people Mary had ever met. She was drop-dead gorgeous, but she seemed unaware of that. Mary didn't know her story, but she observed that she was a devoted friend, wife, and mother. She had a feeling Deb was... resilient. She certainly seemed to take everything in stride. Mary hoped they'd become friends.

Deb patted her arm and said, "Sure. Lead the way." Mary could see the sadness and worry in her eyes. That's when she knew there was something really wrong with Gavin. She'd heard, as had everyone else, that he needed medical marijuana, but Mary now suspected Breacher Syndrome was more than just headaches and social anxiety.

As the pair entered the elevator and the doors closed behind them, Deb spoke. "You're just like them, aren't you, Mary?"

"How so?" Mary asked.

"Analytical, logical, detached in some ways," Deb replied, smiling sadly.

"I suppose so. I can usually separate myself from a situation and deduce what's going on. I'm observant." Mary admitted.

Deb smiled sadly. "Then what's this about? It's more than

Gavin is telling me."

Mary nodded. "You deserve to know. But it's not my place to tell you. We can talk about it when we get back." They made their way to the coffee shop and back.

As soon as they entered Declan's office, Deb sat the coffee on the table and looked at Gavin. She shook her head and smiled. Gavin nodded. It had been a test. Gavin had used Deb to test her. She'd been expecting it, but she'd missed it. Now, she was left wondering if she had passed or failed.

During their absence, Dan and Miranda had arrived and were now sitting together on the sofa. Mary passed out the coffees. She looked at her husband and at Gavin. They both looked at her expectantly. "You two want me to deliver my analysis before the Gunny comes? In front of everybody?"

Declan smiled and took her hand. He gave an encouraging squeeze.

Gavin laughed. "I tell her everything, Mary. That's our deal. There are no more secrets. There shouldn't be. Now, I really do need to know what you've pieced together. You're the analyst. Analyze."

"In November, J2 thwarted a terrorist attack in Dublin. Four members of a Bratva faction in two stolen vehicles surrounded and hijacked a bus full of primary school children. The bus had a bomb on board. It was the exact scenario and execution as the attempt in Fredericksburg that you thwarted last June. The bombs were made by a Muslim Brotherhood member and were identical to several smaller attacks in Egypt 15 years ago."

"That bomb in Fredericksburg was about killing Hal... how?" Deb stammered.

"Yes, but it's still connected, Deb. Bombs have distinctive features...a fingerprint if you will. They were definitely constructed by the same person as the bombings 15 years ago. My guess is that the two bus hijackings were both...practice runs.

I think Declan is trying to prevent a larger-scale attack in Egypt at the grand opening of the Grand Egyptian Museum this fall," Mary continued. Declan nodded.

"You think. He hasn't told you?" Deb asked.

"No. He wouldn't be very good at his job if he told me."

"But you're confident…" Deb persisted.

"I wouldn't be very good at mine if I couldn't analyze what's in front of me," Mary replied. "Declan is definitely worried about the Muslim Brotherhood. It was his first thought when someone killed Howard and came after me. He still thinks Theo was not the mastermind behind the threat against us. And Gavin agrees with him," Mary said, looking Gavin directly in the eyes. He nodded, too.

"Why do they think so?" Deb asked.

"There were three files that Charlene wanted me to work on. One was for an American actress's contract to do a commercial in Egypt for Bowen Tobacco. The actress is Kyra Gibbons. She's Shannon's younger sister. The second was for a US company leasing space for a distributor in Cairo. Small Town South Tobacco, a subsidiary of Bowen Tobacco. The lease was signed by Sean Bowen in June of last year, just after the bus incident," Mary said in a whisper.

"But Gil was in Sterling. He was posing as Sean," Miranda whispered back.

"I suspect the picture taken of Sean at the convenience store was the real Sean, not Gil," Mary continued. Deb and Miranda gasped. "The third file is for an American student who was arrested in Giza for shoplifting back in 2018. The student was Amber Guthrie."

"I still don't understand how the attempt in Dublin is connected to these files, though," Deb continued.

"Don't you? Declan was the agent that thwarted the Dublin attack. And he's named as the lawyer on all three case files. Even though he wasn't with this firm, and it's not his signature," Mary explained. Declan kissed the hand he held.

"Aye, ye've got it. Except for one detail," he said, kissing her hand again.

She turned and looked at him. "I love you, Declan," she chuckled. "You're not so sure that it's Sean who signed the lease and Kris that Mr. Davis shot two years ago. Sean had the scar removed during his 8 years in hiding."

"Dere it is," Declan said. "And I love ye, too."

Declan took a folder out of his briefcase. He took out a CCTV still shot of a man sitting at a street café. He looked at it and sighed. He held it out to Miranda. "Who is in da photo?"

Miranda took the picture and started to shake. "That's Kris," she said.

Declan looked her right in the eyes. "How do ye know?"

"His ears were slightly higher than Sean's... and there's no scar...and I can just tell. He raped me."

"Dat was taken last month in Cairo," Declan said. Miranda dropped the photo. Declan took out a photo of Kris's body after Sam shot him dead.

Miranda took it and looked dejected. "Oh God. That's Sean...only there's no scar."

"Jesus, Theo never called him Kris. She called him Honey or Baby but never by name," Dan said, shaking his head.

"Ye were under a great deal of stress, what wid a knife to yer throat an all. Ye did na notice dat it was Sean, not Kris because ye expected it te be Kris."

"They were both psychopaths?" Miranda asked. "Wait... so Kris is behind this?"

Dan, meanwhile, had grabbed Miranda by both elbows. Declan knew what had happened. Kris Bowen had raped Miranda in 2013. Two years ago, just before Dan and Miranda's wedding, he had kidnapped Dan's son with Deb and murdered

Deb's mother in a narcissistic, psychopathic rage seeking revenge on Dan for being the sole heir to their shared grandmother's fortune and Miranda for not rolling up into a ball and dying after he had raped her. Miranda let out an audible gasp before stifling her screams, stiffening her spine, and donning a stoic expression. Deb had made her way to stand behind Miranda, obviously expecting what had just occurred. She stooped and hugged her friend's neck. Gavin looked at the floor and drummed his fingers.

"Delta Force Security was founded by former Captain Walter Bowen, USMC. He served from 1980 until 1990, when he was mustered out. He was allowed to resign his commission, but there were questions of his mental stability. He founded DFS in 1991 with his business partner and best friend, Casper Turner, and served as CEO of the agency until he took over as CEO of Bowen Tobacco in 1995 after his adoptive father's stroke," Frank explained. "Casper took over DFS after Walter left, but he and his son Kenny disappeared 9 years ago, about a month before Sean's 'fatal' car accident. Sean was groomed to take over, but Kris became the CEO after the accident."

"No. No. No. Sean's DNA was confirmed in the car accident," Miranda blurted out.

"The DNA evidence was only ever confirmed as a match to being the son of Walter Bowen. There were allegations that Kenny…" Frank's words trailed off.

"So, Sean didn't die in the car accident after all? And he wasn't really Gil? Gil really is Dan's brother, but Sean was alive the whole time Gil was pretending to be him, pretending to be Gil? And he was never the nice one? There was no nice one? They were both evil? And my dad killed Sean, not Kris, in our foyer 2 years ago?" Miranda asked, sadly, shaking.

"That was Declan's fear, yes," Gavin said. "He briefed me a few days ago. I…I just didn't know how to…Red, I was hoping he was wrong." He looked her right in the eyes. "Are you okay?"

he asked. Declan had never seen him look so aggrieved.

CHAPTER 44

Gunnery Sergeant Marshall Craig, a veteran of the war in Afghanistan, having served in the Marines from 2011 through 2021, was led by a shapely dark-haired beauty down a tiled hallway to a cherrywood door at its end. The skirt hugged her hips and rear perfectly. She walked with grace and poise, her back straight, but her arms and shoulders relaxed. She had class, he decided...like a black and white 40's movie star, like Bette Davis or Rita Hayworth.

She opened the door, and he stood face to face with a legend, First Lieutenant Gavin Mahoney, Silver Star recipient. Only, he wasn't a mere first lieutenant. He was a three-star general. He had met the man once, after that skirmish that left Gavin with a three-day gap in his memory, in the field hospital. He'd been nearby when the general had earned that silver star. Even though he was in a different branch of the military, he had nothing but the deepest respect for him. Especially since he'd seen him stand up to the Tyrant.

"Lieutenant! Um, sorry. G...General," he stammered.

The man looked perplexed. As did the Irish Armed Forces Major, who sat behind the desk. The Colonel in the corner barely moved. There was a gorgeous blonde and a gorgeous redhead to complete the hat trick with the gorgeous brunette who had met him at the elevator. A tall, green-eyed man sat beside the redhead. The brunette walked around and sat in the Major's lap.

"Do I know you, Gunny Craig?" the General asked.

"No, sir. B...But I was wwwwounded at the same t...t... time as you. I was at the field hospital when you cleaned Major Hopewell's c...clock," Marshall replied, smiling and saluting.

The general cocked his head and looked amused. "I cleaned Major Hopewell's clock? Please, tell me. I was badly concussed and dosed with benzos. I don't remember. But nothing would make me happier."

Marshall looked around the room. They all looked pleased. "Um. Yeah. The T...T...Tyrant...the major showed up d...demanding to see his nephew, Evan. He was t...told there was no Evan, but he intimidated an orderly and generally acted the ass he is..."

"Was," Gavin interrupted. "I shot him in the head in December."

"Uhhhh. R...really? Okay, was. Anyway. You screamed 'Suckin' sin.'"

"Suykin syn," the civilian male interrupted. "It's Russian for 'Son of a bitch.'"

"Okay. Anyway, the major g...ggggrabbed you by the collar. You pushed him off and punched him right in the nose. It was g...glorious."

The general laughed. "God, I wish I could remember that."

"Barry Magill was the Tyrant?" The Irish officer asked.

"If the Tyrant was Major Hopewell, then yes," Gavin replied.

"The Tyrant?" asked the redhead.

Marshall nodded.

"Major Hopewell was not a popular commanding officer. He was domineering, even for Marine. He had the highest rate of disciplinary actions on his troops in Afghanistan. He was unreasonable," Gavin explained.

"But we didn't ask ye here to talk about Major Hopewell," Declan said. "Have a seat."

Marshall nodded again. And sat in the chair the Major pointed to.

"I'm Major Declan Mahoney," he said, as if Gunny didn't

know already. Okay, he'd go along. "Ye already recognized ma cousin, General Gavin Mahoney. Dat's Colonel Bart Walters dere in the corner." The Colonel gave a wave. "Dis is ma wife Mary, the General's wife Deb...she's also the Colonel's niece...our cousin Miranda, and her husband, Deputy Sheriff Dan Bradley." Wife? But he didn't react.

"You want to know about Delta Force Security?" Marshall asked, looking around.

"We do," the general said. He slowly twisted his wedding ring on his left hand. First, one way. Then the other. His voice was low and even. Gunny chuckled.

"No need for that. I think that the faction of Bratva that CID dismantled a few months back has its claws on DFS. I can't prove it, but I believe that Colonel Boyd was an investor in the company...a silent partner, if you will. He spent a great deal of time at headquarters before his arrest last year. As soon as he was arrested, I made inquiries about who was heading up the investigation, but then my mother was mugged and hospitalized, and my baby sister got into a suspicious car accident. So, I backed off," Marshall found himself saying.

He stared at the General's ring. The man's voice was soft, comforting, melodic almost. "Who else is behind DFS? Off the books..." he asked. Whatever. Let him try the hypnosis. It wouldn't work.

"Off the books? DFS's biggest contract is with Bowen Tobacco. Walter Bowen's young wife would be his heir since Kris Bowen died a few years ago, but since she was involved in Walter's murder, she can't inherit. I heard rumbles that Sean Bowen had survived his car crash 9 years ago and had been living in hiding, but he turned out to be a CID man in Illinois. Still, recently, the rumors have persisted. Then I saw him. In Cairo. I'd gone over as a security detail for an actress. It was weird because she's nobody. A bit actress doing a commercial. But then she met

Sean at a hotel."

The general stopped twisting his ring for a second. His melodic voice sounded...urgent as he asked abruptly, "What's her name?"

"Kyra Gibbons," Marshall said.

General Mahoney slammed his right hand down on the desk, hard. "That's Shannon's sister. Damnit. Max James was engaged to Kris Bowen, Mary. I think she married him. Do you know him?"

"I didn't even know she knew him, Gavin. I swear. Max has a whole life I don't know anything about. I usually can see the big picture. Maybe I just didn't want to know...or she's an amazing liar," the beautiful brunette said.

He stared at her. "Go ahead. Put me under," she said defiantly.

"Are you sure?" he asked.

She nodded.

General Mahoney took out a lighter. He flicked it open. "Look at the flame. Concentrate on the sound of my voice. Watch the flame. Do you know Kris Bowen?"

"I never met him. Max had a boyfriend about 9 years ago she didn't want to introduce me to. She didn't know I knew that. It was only for a few months. I figured she'd introduce me when she was ready. But she stopped seeing him, and I just never brought it up," she said.

The general closed the lighter. The brunette let out a breath. "Do you believe me now?" she asked.

He blinked like she had slapped him. "I believed you. You were telling the truth. I thought you understood that. I put you under for the deeper details, not the truth. I'm sorry you misunderstood," he said. He looked genuinely hurt.

"Oh, Jesus, Gavin. We really need to work on our trust issues with each other," she snorted. "Did you get what you wanted?"

"Yeah. I did," he said, laughing.

Marshall was taken aback by the familiarity and jocularity. He hadn't expected to be meeting a family.

"Why am I here?" he mused quietly.

"I needed ye to walk off dat elevator for what comes next, ma friend," the J2 officer said.

"You needed someone to see me?" Marshall asked.

"No worries, Gunny," said the Colonel in the corner. He smiled. It was kind of creepy. Marshall couldn't tell how old he was…older, but 50s, 60s, 70s? He was so pale and so quiet. Until he spoke, Marshall kept forgetting he was there. When he did speak, Marshall wondered if he was in the same corner. Hadn't he been over there? The Mahoneys didn't seem affected. But the man they had introduced as a deputy sheriff jumped just as much as Marshall did.

"Wasn't he…" Marshall started.

"Yes, he's a vampire," the deputy shivered and then laughed.

The Colonel grinned wickedly and raised a single eyebrow.

"Leave him alone, Frank," the general said, drumming his fingers on the desk.

CHAPTER 45

"So, I obviously haven't figured out what I told you. Can you give me a hint?" Mary asked. Declan's heart broke for her. Mary was so astute, except for when it came to Max. He didn't know why. He just knew Maxine James was her blind spot.

"You told us when Max married Kris Bowen, ma Lovely," he said sadly, taking her hand.

He watched the light in her eyes fade as his words sunk in. She shook her head in denial. Then her phone rang. She looked at the caller ID and collapsed into his arms. He took the phone from her hand and accepted the call, holding her phone to his ear. "Hello, Max. Tell Kris to meet us at da Tomb of da Unknown Soldier at da changin' of da guard at 11:30." He disconnected the call, dropped the phone, and took Mary's face in both his hands. "I did tell ye, ma Lovely. She's na to be trusted. But I am so sorry," he said as the tears welled in her eyes and spilled down her cheeks.

Marshall Craig looked at Declan. "Maxine James?" he asked. "AKA Maxine Janovich, AKA Maxine Bowen? She's the CEO of DFS."

"Maxine lives off her trust fund. She's unemployed..." Mary squeaked.

Mary, ma darlin', think about it," Declan pleaded. "Who recommended ye apply fer dis job when ye moved back here?"

She shook her head. "Maxine did, but I've known her since college, 12 years. How can she have this whole life I don't know about?"

"Ma darlin, ma Lovely, who recommended ye apply to work at Park, Davis, and Feldman eight years ago?" he pleaded again, placing his hands on her shoulders.

Huge sobs escaped as she began to hyperventilate. "I…I…I…ttttt…alked to her nearly every day. Shhhhh…eee… was using me ttttt…to spy on Mike and Miranda? Oh, Gawd!"

Frank nodded. "I have things to do," he stated. "I'll see you all later." He glided out of the room.

"That guy is really c…creepy," Marshall noted. Dan nodded furiously.

Miranda took a moment but recovered her composure quickly. Declan had to admire his pretty cousin's character. She looked very much like Gavin's sister, Molly, come to think of it. Same shaped face and eyes, same nose. Molly was darker with nearly black hair, but the resemblance was strong. Gavin looked more like his mother. Like Molly, Miranda possessed an heir of dignity and inner strength that was admirable.

Declan whispered, "I'm…I'm sorry. Dat was cruel."

Gavin, who was still looking at the floor, nodded. "This is the part I hate. This is the version of me I hate."

Miranda stiffened. She took a sharp intake of breath. She breathed out through her nose. She stomped her foot and crossed her arms over her chest. "Get over yourselves! Telling me that Kris is alive and still out to get me is not equivalent to being Kris. Yes, I am going to feel horror being told this. No, it is not you causing that horror. Understand?" she admonished them sternly.

Declan burst out laughing. It was a nervous laugh, but it was cathartic. Soon, everyone was laughing. Laughter was preferable to the pain and fear.

The time arrived, and they all made their way to Arlington National Cemetery. As the ceremony for the changing of the guard began, Declan, Gavin, and Marshall removed their hats and stood silently at attention, with their hands over their hearts throughout. They did not move. They barely blinked. A troop of cub scouts attended and were just in front of the group. As the ceremony ended, a wolf scout turned and stared at the soldiers behind them. He tugged on his dad's sleeve. His dad, Declan noted, had stood at attention just as they had done. He pointed, and his father turned to look. He was clearly active-duty military as he snapped to attention and saluted the general standing silently behind them. Gavin returned the salute and winked at the wolf cub scout. "Are they real soldiers like you, Dad?" the little boy whispered.

"Yes, Stevie. That man is a General. And do you see that ribbon there? That means he has been awarded a Silver Star. He's a hero. The other man is not an American soldier. Irish, I think. He appears to be a major. He was very respectful."

"He saved my life. He's a hero," Gavin said.

"Is he really, though?" came the man's icy voice.

Dan grabbed Miranda around the waist as her knees buckled at the sound of his voice.

"Bona fide. He even rescues kids from terrorists," Gavin said.

"Well, he's not alone in that area, is he?" the man returned. "Where's Theo?"

"Morgue," Gavin replied, turning to face the man.

"Really? Who killed her?" Kris Bowen continued.

"Dat would be me," Declan replied, smiling coldly.

"I guess I should have warned her you were no ordinary lawyer," Kris retorted.

"If ye had dat foreknowledge, ye should 'ave taken heed yerself," Declan said, cocking his head. "Hello, Maxine... Charlene." The two women were standing on either side of Kris.

"Mr. Craig, you should be ashamed of yourself...but it doesn't matter what you've told them. It won't leave Arlington," Kris smirked.

Declan laughed. "Do ye think he's here to blow da whistle? Da whistle was blown last night, ye freak o' nature. Right about now, Federal agents are dismantling DFS offices. He's here te draw ye here," Declan laughed.

Kris's face fell. "What?" he asked.

"Well, ye and yere traitorous bitch of a wife," Declan said. He could feel Mary tense up beside him. Without looking, he knew she was glaring at Max. Max was certainly glaring at her.

"You just couldn't stay away from him. He was the perfect patsy," Max accused her.

"Max, you still don't understand who he is, do you?" Mary laughed.

"My wife can be somewhat shortsighted," Kris confirmed.

"Dat's alright, ma Lovely, I do na mind," Declan laughed again. "She'll know soon enough." He took a step forward. "Charlene killed Howard. Somehow, she figured out he was an ATF agent. Sabah was loyal to the brotherhood. She figured out that ye were in dis fer yer own reasons. It was probably Sherry's boyfriend who shot her. Somehow, Charlene figured out that Mary worked for Howard, so ye tried to get her at da same time dat ye took out Sabah....Fortunately, I was dere. So, ye missed yer chance. Ye decided ye'd let Theo take care of all us, so Max took da chislers to Meghan and John and kept up da best friend act." He took another step forward.

"It doesn't matter now," Kris returned. "We have the cemetery surrounded."

Gavin's phone beeped. He held up the message for everybody to see. The text read "Clear."

"Sorry te disappoint...but na really," Declan said as federal agents swarmed and took the three into custody.

CHAPTER 46

Declan pulled the Mercedes into the driveway of the old Victorian farmhouse. The moving van and pod followed. They had facilitated the turnover of the Worker's Contract to the Egyptian Grand that morning. Gavin and Deb had donated it, as scheduled.

The law office had been raided at the same time as Delta Force Security offices. Roland Kane had been arrested. He had been working with the Bowens for years. The rest of the employees found themselves unemployed.

Declan had indeed slipped Wade Henson his new business card. He'd also offered Marshall Craig a job at the new Shenanigan Dairy American Cheese Processing Plant and American Operations Headquarters to be located in Sterling, IL.

The information regarding the planned terrorist attack in Cairo was turned over to the Egyptian government. The terrorists were all arrested, and the threat was thwarted.

They received word that Kris and Maxine had been released on bail and disappeared, but their supply of money and resources had been cut off. Eamon had tracked them to the Dominican Republic, where they were stuck for the moment. It was true they couldn't be extradited back to the States, but neither could they leave. They were currently powerless.

With his job done and commission resigned, he was looking forward to spending a month or so in Colonial Beach with his wife and stepkids before moving to Sterling, where the four of them would make a new, normal, happy life together. He was excited about the prospect.

Mary smiled and opened her car door. "Ahhh, I need this,"

she sighed. "I need a break from the craziness."

Declan climbed out from behind the wheel and opened the back driver's side door. Both toddlers rushed him, giggling and clamoring for him to carry them. He laughed and managed to get both of them into his arms but went to his knees and playfully went to the ground. "I surrender!" he exclaimed as Dani and Randy proceeded to climb on him and tickle him. It was glorious.

Mary laughed and came running to his aid, only to be pulled into the pile.

Gavin Mahoney stood over them with his hands in his pockets, laughing. "Having fun?" he asked.

"Pwetty Mister!" Dani exclaimed, abandoning the pile to reach for Gavin. He dutifully picked her up and offered a hand to Declan. Declan grasped it and pulled himself up to standing.

"Hey, Gav. Aye, I was havin' a bit o' craic. Who knew it was dis easy te be happy?" he asked.

"I know. I spent my entire life having happiness ripped away, but now it's as simple as holding my wife's hand or putting my kids to bed at night. Anyway, Deb sent me over to ask you all to dinner. Since she doesn't cook…your choice of restaurant," Gavin laughed. Declan realized it was a good laugh, a real laugh. Gavin was happy, too. Life was good.

Lacynda Mathes is a graduate of Radford University in Radford, VA. She holds a B.A. in English.

She is originally from Oak Grove, VA, in Westmoreland County near Colonial Beach. She graduated from Washington and Lee High School, Montross, VA, in 1986. She attended Randolph-Macon College, studied abroad at Wroxton College in Oxfordshire, England, and ultimately transferred to Radford University, where she completed her degree.

She currently resides in Sterling, IL, with her husband. She is the mother to their teenage sons, the eldest with special needs, who has been diagnosed with Lennox Gestaut Syndrome, a catastrophic childhood epilepsy, and severe autism.